REMI
BONE

ALSO BY WILLIAM L. MYERS, JR.

Standalone Psychological Thriller

Backstory

Philadelphia Legal Series

A Criminal Defense

An Engineered Injustice

A Killer's Alibi

A Criminal Justice

REMI BONE

A PSYCHOLOGICAL THRILLER

WILLIAM L. MYERS, JR.

OCEANVIEW (PUBLISHING
SARASOTA, FLORIDA

ISBN 978-1-60809-627-5

Published in the United States of America by Oceanview Publishing

Sarasota, Florida

www.oceanviewpub.com

10 9 8 7 6 5 4 3 2

This book is my homage to the great Elmore Leonard, and to his style of writing. No hooptedoodle.

REMI
BONE

CHAPTER ONE

"TICK TOCK SAYS THE CLOCK. Time's up, mother..."

He says the words.

He pulls the trigger.

The bullet punches Harold Roseman, M.D. against the seat-back. After a moment, his shoulders slump, but he remains seated behind his desk, head back, eyes open.

He lowers the gun to his side, watches the crimson stain spread like ink across the drug doctor's white pinpoint oxford.

He turns and leaves.

From beneath the desk, a gagging sound. A muffled cry.

CHAPTER TWO

REMI BONE STEERS HIS F-150 onto the wide driveway and sees Kayla waiting for him on the steps of the high school. She shoots him the big smile that melts his heart every time. He watches her rise from the steps, tall with long legs, though strong, not like a pelican anymore, the pre-teen gawky stage well behind her now that she's seventeen.

"You're five minutes late," she says in the same mildly scolding tone her mother, his wife, had used on him when she wasn't really mad, just pretending to be, but making a point because it had to be made.

"All the time in the world, at your age, and yet so impatient," he says.

"I'm starving. Let's go to the diner."

Ten minutes later, Remi pulls the truck off Baltimore Avenue into the parking lot, the huge neon sign announcing, "Empire Diner."

They ask for a booth, Remi out of breath by the time they reach it.

"You have to start working out," Kayla says.

"Working out." He rolls his eyes.

"Seriously. You're thin but you have no muscles. You look like Billy Bob Thornton, on that *Goliath* show on Amazon. And you're always huffing and puffing. You need some serious cardio. You should join a gym."

"I'd be too busy staring at women's behinds to get anything done."

"And that's another thing. You really need to start dating. Find yourself a girlfriend."

"Here we go."

"It's been more than four years since Mom's passed. It's time, Remi." Calling him by name, instead of dad or pop, like she has since the first time they met, eleven years before.

He sighs.

"I'm going to put you onto one of those computer dating sites. How about match.com. Or, what's that one for old people? OurTime.com."

"*Out of time.*com."

"You're impossible. You know that?"

"What your mother always said."

They order and eat, him with his giant, dirty-nailed mechanic's hands, her with her long teenage fingers. Father and daughter. Making small talk about their days. Trading snide comments. Her pulling out her cellphone every two minutes and him telling her to put it away.

"Any word yet?" he asks, no need to be more specific because she knows what he's talking about. College applications. They've both been on pins and needles for weeks.

Kayla shakes her head, stuffs the rest of her burger into her mouth.

Remi watches her chew. "I don't know how you stay so thin, the way you eat."

"It's called exercise. You may remember that concept from earlier in our conversation."

"And a hundred conversations before that."

"Don't get smart with me, Remi Bone."

Remi smiles. Another thing her mother always said.

*   *   *

The truck now parked in the driveway, Remi opens the door to their house. A two-story brick affair, seventeen hundred square feet on a quarter acre, a nice flat parcel with a big tree out front and two more in the back. Just enough for a family of three, two since Beatrice passed.

He's hardly into the kitchen when Kayla brushes by him, sits down at the table, and rifles through the mail she retrieved from the mailbox. Bills and junk mail she tosses like a dealer throwing cards at a blackjack table.

Remi, watching, waiting, sees her stop, a white envelope in her hand. She looks up at him now, her eyes nervous. She takes a deep breath, carefully opens the envelope. She reads the letter, both pages, then reads it again. Her eyes widen, fill with tears. He knows what that means, reaches down for her at the same time she jumps from her chair and hugs him.

"I'm in! I'm in!"

They whoop and holler. Then Remi takes the letter. "Congratulations," he says, the first word on page one. He can feel Kayla watching him plod through the letter, watching his eyes move back and forth, watching his lips mouth the words.

"You did it, baby. Your moon shot."

"My moon shot." Admission to the University of Pennsylvania. An Ivy League college. A one-in-a-million chance for a girl from her high school, which isn't one of the best in the state, isn't one with teachers who help students write their essays or point them to professionals who can, isn't one that sponsors the phony travel-abroad-to-help-the-third-world summer humanitarian junkets the top-tier universities favor as evidence of a strong social conscience.

Remi knew all that going in; so did Kayla, when she submitted her admissions package. They talked about it, Remi telling her it didn't matter, none of it, when it came to a girl with a brain smart enough to earn a 4.0 GPA and SAT scores of 1570 and 1590. "A girl with the drive of a freight train," he said and they'd both smiled.

But, of course, it did matter, in the real world, the one outside their little brick house. Where connections and legacy admissions played a part. And yet, somehow . . .

"I'm in." Kayla says it again, pinching herself with the words to see if she'll wake up from a dream.

Remi's about to suggest they go out again, for an ice cream sundae to celebrate, something he's done with her since she was little. But he catches himself, knowing that's not what she wants to do right now.

"Go on upstairs," he says. "Burn up that cellphone telling all your friends."

She hugs him and races up the steps, disappears into her bedroom.

Remi sits at the table. He closes his eyes and begins his inventory. There's still $35,000 left from Beatrice's life insurance. On top of that, he's been squirreling away about 5K a year since Beatrice died. With tuition at $50,000, he has enough for the first year if Kayla lives at home. But she'll want to live on campus, he knows that, and he wants it for her, and that's another fifteen grand a year. He's going to have to pick it up at work. Scrimp to save more. Then, he'll start borrowing against the house. There's a hundred thousand in equity he can pull out.

It'll be tight, but he knows he can make it work. The one thing he doesn't want for Kayla is to leave school a couple hundred thou in debt. That's just too big a hole to climb out of. A mortgage without a house.

He promised Kayla, next to Bea's casket, that he'd take care of her. Making sure she didn't start life choking on debt would seem to be a big part of that.

CHAPTER THREE

LAUREN DEVEREUX, chief of staff to the honorable Wallace Brown, mayor of Philadelphia, watches him lean across his desk in his walnut-paneled office on the second floor of City Hall. "This is unacceptable," he says, poking the copies of the *Philadelphia Inquirer* with his thick index finger.

"Look at this article from Sunday's paper: 'More Than Half of City Murders Unsolved.' It says we had 277 murders last year, and only 45 percent were solved. And on today's front page, we have 'Drugs and Death in Rittenhouse Square.'"

The drug story is about a resurgence of heroin-related deaths and crime. The year before, fifty people died in Philadelphia over a two-week period from heroin laced with fentanyl and a synthetic painkiller known as W-18. The drug deaths occurred in the "Bad-lands," an area encompassing the Kensington and Fairhill sections of the city. Although people in those areas were up in arms about the heroin problem, no one in Center City's office towers had raised an eyebrow.

That was all changed now because of what had been happening in Rittenhouse Square, the iconic seven-acre park five blocks west of City Hall bordered by one of the city's toniest neighborhoods.

"I can't believe this," the mayor says. "A guy dead of an overdose in the middle of Rittenhouse Square. Found two nights ago sitting against the base of the lion statue, dead and wide-eyed. And last night? A drugged-out berserker pulls a taxi driver from his cab and races the car around the park.

"I was woken up at three thirty this morning by a phone call from Louis Alan, the real estate developer. Told me he couldn't walk through the park to get to his eight-million-dollar condo because the police had the whole square cordoned off with yellow tape. He told me they were loading a dead body into an ambulance."

"What is Louis Alan doing out at three thirty in the morning?" The police commissioner looks puzzled. "Isn't he, like, eighty years old?"

Lauren watches the mayor close his eyes and take a deep breath. Wallace Brown doesn't suffer fools well.

"You're missing the point," says Brown. "We can't have people dying of heroin in Rittenhouse Square, or getting mugged. Or *run* over by goddamned taxicabs."

Lauren's mind is on another point, not mentioned by her boss, but very important: that the press is blaming the mayor for both the unsolved murders and the epidemic of heroin deaths, the editorializing chipping away at his already-low poll numbers.

The commissioner shifts in his seat. "I hear you, Mayor. And we're working hard. We got a strike force—a whole squad of detectives devoting full time to the heroin problem. As for the unsolved murders, the police can't be blamed for that. First off, all the stories these days about police brutality are ruining what little credibility we have in the minority communities. And even without that, you know this town has a 'no-snitch' tradition older than Independence Hall. Plus, a lot of the killings are gang-related, and no one wants to cross those people. The fact is, witnesses just don't come forward."

Lauren and the mayor exchange glances. The commissioner is a master of excuses.

"And don't forget, we arrested those six dealers last month. Their preliminary hearings are coming up, and we have an ace in the hole: an associate of theirs who's going to testify against them."

"Yet people are still dying of heroin." The mayor pokes the newspaper again. "But now, it's right downtown, in the business district."

"It's that damned fentanyl." The commissioner shakes his head.

Lauren and the mayor look at each other again, their eyes sending the same message: *Really? So, the fentanyl is ruining the heroin, which, without the opioid is, what, Dr Pepper?*

Wallace Brown waves the commish out of his office and sits back in his big leather chair. Lauren stands and walks to the minibar on the other side of the room. She senses the mayor's eyes follow her the whole way. When she bends to pour his scotch, she feels his x-rays burning through her skirt.

She was friends once with one of Brown's secretaries, now gone. They went out drinking one time and the girl, Tanya, got trashed. Told her how, when they had sex, the mayor preferred to take her from behind, doggie-style. Liked to smack her on the butt when he was doing it. Smack her hard. "You like that?" he'd say. "You like that?"

She'd heard worse things about Wallace Brown, dark rumors. True or not, he's a pig. But a pig on the rise. According to the pundits, he has a good shot at the governor's seat. If the murders and heroin don't derail his reelection as mayor.

"Here," Lauren says, handing him the booze. "It's five o'clock somewhere." Stealing from the Alan Jackson / Jimmy Buffett duet.

A vapid line, but Brown loves it. She sits and watches her boss. Wallace is a good-looking man. Tall, fit. Late forties. Nice teeth. Charming when he wants to be. She'd been tempted, when she first started working for him. Then Tanya gave her the lowdown.

Wallace swallows the last of the scotch. "I'm starving. You want to grab something at Capital Grill?"

"I really wish I could, boss, but—"

"Butcher and Singer? Union League?"

"—that would be great, but I have a doctor's appointment."

She watches the mayor study her a minute. He frowns, then waves her out.

CHAPTER FOUR

LYING ON HER SIDE on the California king bed, Lauren looks through the windows at the bright yellow clock on City Hall tower. It reads 8:00 p.m. She hears the toilet flush in the adjoining bathroom. After a minute, Nick Loughead, Esquire, opens the door and strolls naked across the room, to the windows. Gazing down at Dilworth Plaza, he says, "They did a nice job fixing up that shithole. It was mostly federal stimulus money, you know? And five mil from the Ritz."

"That's what I heard," Lauren says, the sex being over only a few minutes ago, and already annoyed with herself for sleeping with him. They'd been doing this on and off for years, since law school. Even when both were seeing other people.

Nick, reading her mood, says, "What? Already?"

"I don't know why I do this. I hate myself as soon as we're done."

"I don't make demands, is why."

She shrugs. He's right. Even when he was single, he never pushed to be her boyfriend, didn't even want to go out on dates. Just sex.

"Plus, I'm the best you've ever had."

He's right about that, too. The shit. Not that she'd ever admit it to him. His ego's big enough already.

"So, whose place is this?" Lauren asks. Nick lives in Bryn Mawr with his wife, Amy. Nick showed her a picture once, Amy being a little frumpy, but sweet-looking. *I really hate myself.*

"A client."

"That's what I figured. Or that basketball player you know."

Nick starts to dress, and Lauren thinks, as she often has, that he's the only guy over forty she's ever known who looks better naked than dressed. Of course, a big part of that is because he buys his suits off the sale rack at Today's Man. Cheap suits that fit poorly. Why he doesn't upgrade to Boyds, or even Joseph A. Banks, is beyond her. He makes enough money. Or claims to.

Nick lowers himself to the bed to put his socks on. He stares at his feet for a moment, then sits up.

"I've never noticed before, but I have beautiful toes."

She rolls her eyes.

"Seriously," he says, lifting his foot. "Look at that big toe. Tell me that's not something."

She glances at the toe, which is actually rather unattractive, and more than a little crooked.

"There's something not right with you."

He seems to think on this a moment, then shrugs. "I have to get going," he says. He puts on his socks and shoes then stands and walks to the window where he uses his reflection to knot his tie. "Amy's parents are going out for an early dinner near our house and are coming over for drinks afterward."

Lauren throws her legs over the bed, stands, and gathers her clothes.

"You can stay if you want," Nick says. "But if a seventy-five-year-old wise guy who looks like a walking skeleton comes in toting a couple of long-legged bimbos, you'll have to fix them some drinks. Maybe join in."

CHAPTER FIVE

NICK LOUGHEAD LEAVES the Ritz and walks the three blocks to his office on Fifteenth Street, just north of City Hall. It's a second-story walk-up above a karate studio. Nick likes that he has a place where no one knows who comes to see him; a tower office wouldn't suit him at all.

Amy and her parents can wait a few more minutes, he decides. He has business to conduct. He slides his iPhone into his breast pocket and pulls his burner from the drawer. He starts dialing but before he finishes, his landline rings.

"Is this Mr. *Lauffhead*?" the caller asks. "The lawyer?"

"It's pronounced *Law*-Head."

There's a pause at the other end, then, "You do criminal defense, right? You handled my cousin Hector's case. Hector Martinez?"

"Maybe. Who's this?"

"Hector's cousin. I just said that."

Nick sighs. "What's your name, and what do you need a lawyer for?"

"Oh. This is Luis Galarza. They got me on possession with intent to sell."

"How much, of what?"

"Twenty ounces. Weed. Allegedly."

"That's serious," Nick says.

"You're telling me. I've been upstate twice already."

"The retainer's $2,500. I bill $250 an hour against it. Once I've exhausted the retainer, you'll have to give me another $2,500. Cash. All cash."

"Cash, yeah, what Hector said. So you don't have to pay taxes on it."

"I report every cent I bring in," Nick insists, thinking it's closer to a third.

"When can I come see you?"

"How about tomorrow, two p.m."

"I'll be there. Do I have to bring the money with me?"

"What do you think?"

Nick hangs up and smiles. "Cha-ching."

There are a 169 gangs involved in the Philadelphia retail drug trade. He's represented members of about forty of those gangs. Luis' cousin Hector is with a Puerto Rican crew selling near B and Indiana in the Fairhill section of the city. Luis must be with the same outfit.

Drug gangs are Nick Loughead's meat and potatoes. They provide a steady stream of income, and he thanks God every day for them. What he really prays for, though, is to get a big break with the Dominican organizations that do the wholesaling. The Dominicans drive a lot more product, have a lot more money, and can afford a whole lot more in legal fees than the Hectors and Luises of the world.

Dialing on his burner phone, Nick is convinced he's on the cusp of the break he's looking for. A few months earlier, a street hustler named Oliver "Rolli" Castillo was arrested with a pound of heroin on him. Castillo traded the charges for the location of a Dominican stash house and the timing of a major shipment into the same.

The police raided the place and arrested six Dominicans, who now awaited preliminary hearings. Because Rolli's tip was the sole basis of the raiding officers' affidavit of probable cause, the magic ticket that secured the search warrant that gave the cops legal authority to storm the warehouse, his testimony at the preliminary hearings will be critical.

All of which means that Rolli Castillo has to go away, about which Nick Loughead has made certain promises to Jabes Santana, one of the Dominican group's higher-ups. Jabes is on the phone now.

"You find someone to do the job yet?" asks Jabes.

"I'm working on it."

Air on the other end of the line.

"Don't worry, I'm close," Nick says. "It's just, like I said before, it can't be one of my clients. Has to be someone who can't be tied to me. Makes it a little harder."

"You want to work with us, you got to make your bones," Santana says, using a phrase from a mobster flick.

"Come on, Jabes, I've been doing your laundry for almost a year," referring to his helping Santana's group launder money through his law firm, having them pay him giant "legal fees" then giving the money back.

"That's just a basic service. Like free checking. You want to rep us in court, rake in the big fees, you got to step up. Like I explained."

"I'm not complaining. Just asking for a little more time. I'll get it done. Believe me."

"Believe me." Jabes chuckles. "You sounding like the president."

Nick hangs up the phone and makes another call. "Hey, Uncle Deke," he says. "It's Nick."

"Nicky boy, how you doing?"

"Any luck yet, getting me a guy?"

"Don't worry," Deke says. "I thought about it and I know who I'm going to ask."

"You haven't talked to him yet?"

"Guy did hard time. Plus, he served in the Middle East, never talks about it. Never brags. That tells me he did some serious shit over there. Those're the guys who don't go on and on about it, the ones who shot people up."

"I need an answer soon," Nick says. "I'm getting pressure on the other end."

"Why don't your guys just do it themselves?"

"Same reason I'm coming to you, instead of asking one of my clients. They don't want any connection to it, no way the cops can trace it back."

"Don't sound right to me, them being afraid of the law. You sure there isn't something else going on?"

"There's nothing more," Nick says.

"A Dominican ready to pay 25K to ice a street hustler?"

"I'm telling you that's all there is to it."

"How's Amy?"

"Doing great."

"My favorite niece."

"My favorite wife." *Not.*

CHAPTER SIX

REMI STANDS BACK to admire his work. The 454 horsepower 4.7-liter V8 engine in the Maserati Gran Turismo Sport is growling sweetly now. The investment banker who handed the keys to Remi will be happy. And it was Remi, personally, not Deke Buford, his boss, to whom the slick-haired money boy entrusted his baby.

Remi works for Deke at Buford's Garage, a dingy, two-story brick building just off of Baltimore Avenue in southwest Philadelphia. Four bays with hydraulic lifts, two garage doors opening onto a cracked macadam lot surrounded by a cinderblock wall topped with razor wire. It's not the best of neighborhoods. But when a man has a special skill, like Remi, word gets around. So it's not unusual to see Maseratis, Lamborghinis, Bugattis, even a Rolls parked in the Buford's Garage compound.

"Worked your magic again," Deke says over Remi's shoulder.

"Took a while."

"Two hours. We'll bill him for five." Deke slaps Remi's shoulder. "Plus parts. And more parts."

"That kid beats this car into the ground." Remi shakes his head.

"Repeat business," Deke says, moving closer.

Remi turns away and scrunches his nose, but not fast enough to avoid inhaling Deke's fetid breath. Sour milk over rancid poultry.

"Come see me after we close," Deke says. "I got a proposal for you."

"A proposal? As in a nice fat raise?"

Deke chuckles and walks away.

Remi turns in time to see Deke enter his cramped office and close the door. Strange man, Remi thinks. Claims to have been a NASCAR racer when he was young. Says Richard Petty made him crash one time, early in their careers, that if Petty hadn't pulled the dirty move, he'd have won the race and *he* would have been Richard Petty. Remi figures it's all bullshit. Much of what Deacon Buford says is bullshit.

Remi lifts his personal toolbox, but he's only able to carry it a few steps before he gets out of breath and has to set it down. *Damn.* The shortness of breath thing has been getting worse and worse. At least this time, he doesn't feel dizzy. That's been happening a lot, too. He knows something's wrong, has been for a while. His family doctor confirmed it a few weeks back. Had him sent for an MRI or a CT scan; Remi can't remember which. When the results came back, he called Remi and told him to consult with a specialist.

He figures the doc'll tell him he needs a stent. He'll lose a day or two of work. That's what happened with Barry, one of the other mechanics. Doctors said he had a blockage and put a little metal cage inside one of his arteries.

*   *   *

A few hours later, when he and Deke are the only ones left, Remi knocks on the door to the office. Deke tells him to come in and close the door behind him.

Remi sits on a metal folding chair in front of Deke's gunmetal gray desk. "So. This proposal."

Deke lifts a cigarette and clicks open his Zippo and lights it. He takes a deep drag and blows out a cloud of smoke. It irritates Remi's eyes, but he says nothing because he doesn't want Deke to know it's gotten to him.

"You hear about all the problems they're having with heroin? High-school kids dying of overdoses?"

Remi's heard the news reports, but doesn't answer.

"It's happening right here in Philadelphia. Our own city."

"I know where we live."

"Seems no one's doing anything about it."

Remi stares, wondering where Deke is headed.

"What if you could do something about it? You and me? Would you be up for that?"

"Cut to the chase, Deke. Kayla's at basketball practice, and I gotta pick her up in an hour."

"See, now, that's what I'm talking about. Your daughter's in high school. She may as well have a bullseye on her."

"Kayla's a straight-A student. And she don't do drugs. You're starting to piss me off, Deke."

Buford raises his hands. "I'm not accusing her. I'm just saying you and me have a chance to do something, maybe save some kids Kayla's age, maybe even one of her classmates, from this goddamn plague."

Remi sighs and feels his heart skip. Another thing that's been happening. "The hell are you talking about?"

"Well, a guy I know, a friend of mine, knows of a guy goes around selling heroin spiked with fentanyl. Selling to kids. And the fentanyl is what's killing them."

"What's that have to do with me?"

"My friend knows some other guys ready to pay good money, big money, to make this prick go away."

"That doesn't answer my question."

"Well, I mean, I know you done some hard time, is all."

Remi stares but doesn't say anything.

"And you were in the Middle East—what was it called? Desert Storm?—and you never talk about what you done there, which tells me you done some things, all right."

"You're not getting any closer to answering my question," Remi says. "Not one step."

"Well—"

"Why in hell are you thinking about getting involved in something like this yourself? You own your own business. You're eighty years old."

Deke leans back in his chair. "Remember last year that guy owed us all that money for the work we did on his Ferrari?"

"All the work I did."

"He wouldn't pay and he wouldn't pay. And then, all of a sudden, he paid."

"You sicked some muscle on him?"

"My friend did. So, now I owe him."

"So why can't your friend call up the guys who beat on Ferrari boy?"

"He can't get anywhere near this. One of his guys does it, and gets caught, leads right to him."

Remi leans forward. "I ought to kick your ass right now. I got a daughter, man. And I don't like how it seems like you see me."

"Hey." Buford raises his hands. "I didn't mean anything by it. It's just a proposal, you know, for you to think over."

"Nothing to think over. I ought to go back and work for Eurocoach."

Remi stands and Deke shoots out of his chair, follows him out of the office. "Come on, man. I'm sorry. Listen, I'll—"

Still walking away, Remi flicks his hand, signaling Deke to shut up.

A few minutes later, in his pickup, Remi turns up the radio and shakes his head. Tomorrow morning, he knows, he'll find an envelope in his toolbox with two hundred cash in it. Deke's normal bribe for when he's pissed off one of his employees by doing something really stupid. He'll take the two hundred then maybe he'll give a call to Big Dave at the Eurocoach in Berwyn. The shop was a lot nicer; the owner was a whole lot nicer. But Deke's place is closer to home and Kayla's high school. Deke paid more, too, and Remi needs to make, and save, as much as he can, to pay for Kayla's college.

"Damn." He knows he isn't going to call Big Dave. Still, *there better be two Cs in my toolbox.*

CHAPTER SEVEN

REMI STUDIES THE DOCTOR, looking for signs of what's coming. He remembers the doctor, Paxton, from high school. Smart-ass kid, Chucky Paxton, always cracking wise, making jokes about people like he was smarter than them, which it turned out he was. A cardiologist now, going by Charles Paxton, III, M.D., and living in a mansion on the main line, with his third or fourth wife, Remi's heard. Paxton was on the list of specialists Remi's family doctor gave him. Remi told Paxton's staff he grew up with him, but it still took a month to get an appointment.

Remi sits across the desk from Chuckie, now with a nose fat and red with broken blood vessels, and stained teeth and fingertips. A heavy drinker. Heavy smoker.

Staring down at the films and papers on his desk, the doctor talks about a weakened heart muscle, ejection fractions, high blood pressure, and diabetes as contributing factors. He drones on for five minutes before Remi interrupts.

"Do you remember me?" Remi asks.

"You were that skinny kid in high school with the big shoulders and giant fists who was always getting into fights. You beat me up. Three times."

"I don't remember that, but you're probably right."

They look at each other for a minute, until Remi says, "So what's the bottom line? In English."

"You have congestive heart failure, late stage."

"English."

"A bum ticker. You're heart's a piece of junk."

"I'm only fifty-one," says Remi, trying to talk the doctor out of it.

"Fifty-one. With a history of high blood pressure and diabetes. And now, congestive heart failure."

Remi's shoulders slump. "Well. Fuck-a-doodle-doo."

Chuckie Paxton reaches for a bottle of water, takes a sip.

"You said 'late-stage.' What's that mean?"

"You ever watch *Breaking Bad*?"

"Sure. So what?"

"Time to start cooking the meth."

They sit for a minute, then the doctor tells him there's little to do but wait for a heart transplant. Says he'll put him on the list.

"How long's this list?"

"You got a will? You should see a lawyer."

Remi's mind flashes to Kayla, to the time she was thirteen years old and standing next to him at the burial of her mother, his wife, Beatrice. And Kayla looked up at him, her eyes filled with tears, and fear. "Who's going to take care of me?" And he said, "I will." And he meant it. And he had. But now what?

Remi stands and walks to the door. He turns around. "You know what? You have a terrible bedside manner."

"You sound like my wife."

CHAPTER EIGHT

DETECTIVE ED "NO RELATION" Rizzo sits across the metal desk he shares with his partner, Patrick Flynn. At fifty-four, Rizzo has thick silver hair and a broad face with wide-set brown eyes. Heavy moving to fat, he walks with a slight limp thanks to a bullet that grazed his thigh bone twenty years before.

"Damn lieutenant," Rizzo says. "Reaming us out like it's our fault there's a heroin epidemic. Our idea to lace it with fentanyl." Rizzo says the words, but he's not all that upset. He knows the lieutenant came down hard on him and Flynn because the captain came down hard on the lieutenant because the chief kicked the captain because the commissioner stomped on the chief because the mayor lowered the boom on the commish. The universal downward flow of blame in all highly evolved human organizations.

Flynn shakes his head, agreeing without saying so. Fresh off patrol, Flynn, a clean-cut twenty-five-year-old, is brand new to Narcotics, where he was conscripted onto the heroin task force.

Flynn has closely cropped blond hair, thick arms from lifting weights, and an already well-developed beer gut. He stands, tells Rizzo, "I'll be back in a minute."

Nodding toward Flynn's midsection, Rizzo says, "You should read the label before you light up. Says smoking's dangerous for pregnant women."

Flynn pauses, then smiles, cups his hand by his crotch. "Eat me."

"Keep disrespecting me like that, you might actually make it around here."

A few minutes after Flynn leaves, Rizzo gets a call from the district attorney's office. Rizzo, his fists clenched, listens for a while, then says, "I don't know why you let that little shit out on the street to begin with. That was a dumbass thing to do. You should've kept him locked up until the preliminary hearings."

"He wasn't going to talk unless we cut him loose," the assistant district attorney says at the other end. "You know that. You sat in with him and his mouthpiece when we negotiated the deal."

"And now he's walking around with a target on his back. Or a plane ticket to Puerto Rico."

"He's not going anywhere. Both of his brothers are facing charges of their own, and Castillo knows we'll throw the book at them if he skips. And he'd be a lot more vulnerable inside."

Rizzo sighs. "I'll find him, bring him in to talk to you."

"You know where he is?"

"I know someone who does."

Rizzo hangs up just as Flynn returns from his cigarette break.

"Who was that?" Flynn asks.

"DA's office. Seems Rolli Castillo's gone AWOL. The DA wants us to fetch him for a sit-down."

"They worried he left town? They'd be up the creek at the preliminary hearings without him. Those other six would walk."

"Nobody's walking. Come on."

Rizzo leads Flynn to the car, takes shotgun.

"Where to?" asks Flynn.

"Just go up 95."

*　　*　　*

Half an hour later, Rizzo has Flynn turn the car off Kensington Avenue onto East Somerset. A few blocks down, they turn again and park in front of a beat-up brick row-house, done out in chipped white paint. Like most of the houses on the block, the first-floor window is protected by steel bars. Rizzo knocks on the door, Flynn stands on the sidewalk, looking around.

While they wait, a black pit bull ambles up to the step, looks up at Rizzo, and urinates. The dog sits down and licks itself, then slowly makes its way back down the street.

"He didn't think much of you," Flynn says.

Rizzo ignores the remark, knocks again. Hard.

A woman, late twenties going on fifty, opens the door. "Rizzo. Wachu want?"

"Hello, Valeria. I'm looking for Rolli."

"Why you want to see . . . goddamnit! That dog pissed on my house again?"

"I just want to talk to him. He's not in any trouble."

"Since when?"

"Has he given you anything for the rent this month?" Rizzo asks. "How about support, for the kid?"

"You kidding me? I haven't seen him in six months, maybe more."

"You tell me where he is, I'll squeeze him. Bring you the dough myself."

Valeria looks warily from Rizzo to Flynn.

"Come on," Rizzo says. "Tell me where I can find him. I'll be back here in an hour."

"But I just told you. He don't come around here no more."

"Tom Petty."

"Huh?"

"When he did come around, where'd he spend his days?"

Valeria looks up and down the street. "There's a shithole bar about three blocks from here, has a black sign out front with no name on it. Iron gate on the door makes it looks like it's closed down."

"I know it." Rizzo turns to Flynn. "Come on."

"Hey! You're coming back here, right? In an hour?"

"Sure."

On the way to the bar, Flynn says to Rizzo, "She knew who you were as soon as she opened the door."

"Every dirtbag in the Badlands knows me. Or of me."

*   *   *

Rizzo stands in the doorway while his eyes adjust to the darkness, then quickly scans the place. The bar is as nasty on the inside as Rizzo expected of a place whose sign is a piece of painted black wood. Curled-up linoleum flooring. The reek of stale cigarette smoke, cheap beer, and urine from the swampy bathroom.

A morbidly fat bartender with thick stubble stares at him for a minute, belches, then turns away. Two men sit huddled over the bar. Another is asleep on a table.

In the back of the room, in shadows, is a single booth. Rizzo leads Flynn to it, slides in across the table from its sole occupant.

"Your phone broke?"

A sly smile. Predator's eyes. "Detective Ed Rizzo. What brings you to this lovely spot?"

"The DA's been trying to get ahold of you. Needs to see you, shore up your testimony for the preliminary hearings."

"I'll be there."

"I wouldn't be so confident, I were you. You shouldn't be out on the street. I'm surprised you're not in a hole by now," Rizzo says.

Castillo looks around. "A hole? What do you call this place?"

Flynn smiles, looks at Rizzo. "He's got a point."

"I know the DA offered to put you in witness protection until you testified."

"Sit around some hotel room with a pair of cops playing cards, stuffing their faces with cheesesteaks and potato chips? Not my style."

"Uh-huh. You know the rumor is you're still selling. And you left your old lady for a nicer piece you had on the side."

Rizzo watches Castillo smile and lean back. A cool character, this one.

"Not me. I'm on the straight and narrow. And I'm a family man. I have a one-year-old."

"When's the last time you paid Valeria's rent?"

Castillo's smile remains, but his eyes grow a little colder. "I was meaning to drop her off some money—today, in fact. Though, times are tough. 'Specially for someone like me, someone *not* selling."

Rizzo stares. "I'm looking at this booth and I see you sitting here, but I don't see a drink. Tells me you come in here for something else. Like a meeting. Maybe with a supplier. Or some corner boys to hand shit off to."

Castillo's nostrils flair, and he stiffens, just a little, but enough that Rizzo can tell he's exerting effort to control himself.

Switching subjects, Castillo nods toward Flynn. "This your partner? Why doesn't he say anything?"

"He's new," Rizzo says. "We're in the watch and learn phase. This is what you call on-the-job training."

"Philly cops using you as a trainer? They must really be scaling back."

Castillo expects a smile out of Rizzo, but he dead-eyes him. "As an example of me showing him the ropes, this is where I tell you that you have to use the men's room before we leave."

"I don't have to go."

"Really? You want to try'n sneak that piece you have tucked in the back of your pants into the DA's office? Go on now, hide it in the bathroom and come back for it later."

Castillo starts to get out of the booth, and Rizzo says, "Better walk backward. I see the bulge in your backside from that weapon, I'm going to have to seize it."

Castillo's eyes narrow. "You really are an SOB, Rizzo."

Rizzo smiles. "Word on the street."

"How did you know he was carrying?" asks Flynn.

"Same way he knows you and me are carrying. Part of the job description."

When Castillo's done in the restroom, Rizzo and Flynn lead him to the car. Before they get in, Rizzo tells Castillo, "We're going to make a stop before we see the DA." Then he reaches into Castillo's back pocket, lifts his wallet. "Going to see Valeria, so you can give her some rent money."

Rolli clenches his jaw, spits out, "Rizzo."

CHAPTER NINE

REMI ENTERS THE business center building, takes the elevator to the second floor, and walks to the attorney's office at the end of the hall. The lawyer's a solo practitioner, handles wills, family law, divorces, and criminal defense work. "You name it," the lawyer, Dominic Glick, had said when Remi called the day before.

Remi set up the meeting for his lunch hour, and he figures it must be Glick's lunch hour, too, because there's a half-eaten sandwich on his desk. A sandwich and a Diet Pepsi, which, judging by the lawyer's gut, isn't working.

"Sorry about the mess. I have to be in court later this afternoon, so I have to multitask."

Remi says no problem, and the lawyer gets right down to it. "So, tell me what's up. You didn't want to say over the phone. This a criminal thing? You look a little rough around the edges."

Remi shrugs. "I had some problems, when I was younger."

"Guest of the state?"

"A few years. But that's not why I'm here." Remi takes a deep breath and explains what Chuckie Paxton told him about his heart. Says his wife is dead and he's raising their daughter, her biological daughter and his by adoption, and wants to make sure she gets everything he has when he goes.

"No problem. I can do a simple will. Can you give me a little more detail? Your wife, Beatrice—you said her name was—how long were you married? When did she pass? When did you adopt Kayla, who is how old?"

"Kayla is seventeen. I adopted her when she was eight, right after I married Beatrice. We'd met about two years before, when Kayla was six."

The racial thing only came up once between him and Beatrice. It was right after the first time they'd made love. They were lying in bed, looking up at the ceiling. He turned to her.

"You have a problem with me being white?"

"No. You have a problem with me being black?"

"Nope."

"All right, then."

The lawyer asks him, "Did Kayla take your name? Bo-nay? How do you spell that, by the way?"

"B-O-H-N-E. And Bea didn't want her to take my name because everyone sees it and thinks its pronounced *bone*. Like dog bone. Happened to me when I grew up. Everyone called me Remi Bone, and it stuck."

"Remi?"

"Short for Remington. My old man named me after a bolt-action rifle he won a shooting competition with. He thought that was hilarious."

Glick searches Remi's eyes, trying to read what he thinks of the joke, but doesn't find anything. "So, Kayla's last name is Washington, like your wife?"

Remi nods.

"How about the father—"

"I'm the father."

"I apologize. I meant the natural, uh, biological father."

"Not a part of the equation."

"The law might say otherwise."

"No one knows who he is."

"He knows who he is. Has he ever come around, staking a claim? On Kayla, or on Beatrice?"

"Once. A long time ago. But I set him straight." Remi doesn't share the details, that his wife's long-ago abuser had shown up out of nowhere right after he and Beatrice were married and before he'd adopted Kayla. He came home from work to find Beatrice, with a black eye, stewing on the couch. She wouldn't tell him what happened at first but finally admitted to it. The next day, he followed the guy from his office to his parking lot and confronted him. The guy was taller and pretty solid, but he was so pissed, it didn't matter. He clocked him, sent the guy onto his ass. A week later, two cops showed up at his work, stuffed him into an unmarked car, drove him to a field, and beat the shit out of him.

"And you haven't heard from him since?"

"No. And Bea hadn't heard from him for years before that. He'd left her when she was pregnant with Kayla. Never acknowledged his daughter, or that he'd had a relationship with Bea. But she was good with that, because of how he'd treated her. Hitting her. And worse."

Remi's eyes flatten as he glosses over the details. After he and Beatrice had gotten serious, she'd shared the whole horror story with him, to let him know why she had trust issues when it came to men.

"How sure are you that this guy won't show up, try to establish a relationship with your daughter once you're gone?"

The question stops Remi cold. The idea the sadist would make an appearance, tell Kayla he was her father, hadn't entered his mind. Now, it overwhelms it.

"Hey? You okay?"

"Huh, yeah."

"So, what do you think? Any chance he'll come forward?"

"I don't think so." But would he?

"All right. So, let's get to the assets. What do you own?"

"Well, I own my house. There's a mortgage, but I have about 100K in equity. There's thirty-five left from Bea's life insurance, another twenty thousand more in savings. And my truck."

"IRA account? 401(k)?"

Remy's look says: *Are you kidding?*

"How about life insurance?"

Remi closes his eyes, exhales. "Just enough to bury me. Shit. You think I could get more?"

It's the lawyer's turn to shoot the *are you kidding?* "With congestive heart failure?"

Remi sighs.

A few minutes later, Remi leaves having given the attorney a check for $250 for a basic will, which'll leave his assets, such as they are, to Kayla and appoint her as his executrix.

"How soon do you need this?"

Remi remembers Chuckie Paxton's line about cooking the meth.

"Sooner the better."

CHAPTER TEN

REMI CLOSES THE hood of a Lamborghini Huracán Spyder. It's owned by a thirty-eight-year-old plastic surgeon who decided a high-performance sports car with a 610 horsepower V10 engine is the perfect vehicle for the fifteen-mile-an-hour stop-and-go on the Schuylkill expressway. Burned out the clutch in three months.

Remi shakes his head, amazed, as always, that jackasses seem to have a special form of gravity that attracts money.

He sits on the red, molded plastic chair in his car bay and puts his hand to his chest, feeling for his heartbeat. It seems fine. But there's no getting around what Chuckie Paxton told him. Or his shortness of breath, or the dizziness, both getting worse by the week. He knows from firsthand experience that it doesn't take long for the grim reaper to sneak up on you, his wife, Beatrice, being fit as a fiddle on her fortieth birthday, then, a month later, starting to feel pain when she urinated, then starting to bleed when she shouldn't be bleeding, then the doctor saying she had an onion-sized tumor in her uterus, then being told she had stage 4 cancer, then being dead before she reached forty-one.

Remi sits for a long while. He sighs and stands and walks toward Deke's office. His eyes on the old man the whole way, he enters, closes the door, and sits in front of the desk.

"This guy. The one who sells the bad heroin that's been killing the kids. The one that got away. Tell me about him."

Remi watches Deke smile, and his insides roil.

CHAPTER ELEVEN

REMI SITS ON his couch, leaning forward, elbows on his knees, head in his hands. He was supposed to meet with Deke, work out the details of the job, but he called out sick, having a hard time convincing himself to go through with it.

For motivation, he envisions Kayla strolling with other students on Penn's ivy-hung campus, laughing in the sunshine. He imagines her in serious discussions about philosophy, history, literature, art, and whatever else Ivy League students ponder and argue about. He sees her taking trips with her friends to New York City, studying abroad in Paris or China. And it will all be because he, then resting in his grave, had done the hard deeds necessary to open all those doors for her. But he needs to build up her inheritance, because, of course, he will be dead soon.

On that last score, he had called Chuckie Paxton, the conversation going like this:

"I know you explained everything to me, but I just wanted to be sure I heard you right. About how bad my condition is, how much time I have left."

The line was quiet for what seemed to Remi like a long time.

"You still there, doc?"

"Remi, did you ever see that movie with Susan Sarandon? And Sean Penn? Where he's a convicted killer and she's a nun who wants to help him?"

He'd seen the film. *Dead Man Walking.* "Fuck you."

"Again, you sound like my wife."

But Remi didn't hear that as he was already on the way to slamming down the phone.

* * *

To put himself in the right frame of mind to actually do the deed, Remi tries to imagine himself as Samuel L. Jackson, one of the coolest actors of all time, playing Jules Winnfield, one of the coolest hit men of all time. Every time he watches *Pulp Fiction*, he's captivated by the scenes where the unflappable Winnfield recites the biblical passages about the Lord's vengeance and righteous anger. The ones from Ezekiel.

He sees himself doing the job not as Remi Bone, but as Jules Winnfield. He looks in the Bible for a passage to shout at the drug dealer before he shoots him. Something shorter than the Jackson/Winnfield passage, easier to remember. Some that he test-drives in his mind are:

From Ecclesiastes:

To everything there is a season.
A time to give birth, and a time to die.

From Roman's 13:4:

[I]f thou do that which is evil, be afraid; for he beareth not the sword in vain: for he is the minister of God, a revenger to [execute] wrath upon him that doeth evil.

The one he settles on is from Psalm 58, which goes, *The righteous will rejoice when he sees the vengeance; he will bathe his feet in the blood of the wicked.* This seems like it'll be the easiest to commit to memory. And, for purposes of rationalization, he decides that, certainly, a heroin dealer falls within the category of *wicked.*

He stands, his left hand holding his bible, his right hand holding his imaginary gun. He reads the passage, shoots the wicked heroin dealer.

He struggles with it. On the one hand, he loves Kayla, loves her more than anything. And he'd promised he'd take care of her. Promised her next to her mother's grave, Kayla standing there terrified and with a broken heart. An image that comes to him whenever he needs motivation to stay on the straight and narrow.

On the other hand, he doesn't see himself as a bad man, not anymore. He'd done bad things, when he was younger, and then after he came home from the war. But a kid is a kid, and as for the other stuff, he'd served his time, paid his debt. Then he cleaned himself up, learned a trade. Found a fine woman and married her. And he was doing everything he could to raise his girl to become that same kind of woman. All of which made him a good father. Which made him a good man.

But what he's thinking of doing, that's bad. It's wrong to kill. Period.

Isn't it?

* * *

Two days later and he's sitting on the couch.

God, give me a sign.

And then, just as he's begging and pleading, it comes—on TV, anchorman Jim saying, "Police have confirmed to Action News that two students at Overbrook High School died of heroin over-doses early this morning. The names of the students, both juniors, are being withheld until their relatives can be notified."

Remi sits before the television, his ears ringing with the word "relatives," picturing the terrible news sweeping through two families, like a scythe mowing down corn stalks. He sees a drug dealer selling his tainted wares, laughing and dancing, not a care in the world, his identity unknown to the police. He sees the drug dealer, now unsmiling as he sees the gun, and hears the words: "The righteous will rejoice when he sees the vengeance; he will bathe his feet in the blood of the wicked." He sees his arm leading to his hand, his hand gripping the gun. But he still doesn't see himself pulling the trigger.

He stands, finds the Bible, given to Beatrice by her mother, worn from use. He stares at it. Takes a deep breath. Remembers Jesus asking God to take the cup from him, Moses begging God to send someone else to speak to Pharaoh.

He's killed before. In war. And once, in prison. Necessary in both cases, but legal only in one.

He walks to the door and reaches for his coat on the rack. He needs guidance. But he can't go to see the Reverend Jones, Bea's spiritual guide. The reverend was against her marrying him, a former convict, and made no bones about it. He hadn't been to church since Bea's funeral, disliking the man for disliking him. But there's another he can turn to, or hopes he can—not sure because it's been so long, but thinking maybe because the guy ended up a priest. A miracle if ever there was one.

CHAPTER TWELVE

"YOU SIT THERE any longer, I'll have to draw up a lease."

Remi, pulled from his thoughts, looks up at the priest. A big man, going at least two-twenty. White crew cut, clean shaven. Face of leather, cracked and wrinkled. Seeming more ex-military than priest, except for the eyes, kindness rimmed with something Remy can't quite read.

"Not like I'm taking anybody's place," Remi says, looking around the empty church, Holy Redeemer, always in the newspaper as being on the diocese's short list of parishes to close or consolidate.

The big man sighs. "Come on, you look like a man needs to talk."

Remi rises and lets the priest lead him past the altar into the robing room. It's a bare space. Worn hardwood floor, worn wood paneling.

The priest walks behind a bare desk, motions for Remi to take one of the two visitors' chairs. When they're seated, the priest looks at his watch, mutters something Remi thinks is "close enough," then pulls a bottle of Johnny Walker and two tumblers from a bottom drawer. He pours into one, looks at Remi, who shakes his head "no," then pours into the other anyway.

Remi watches the priest empty his glass in one swallow, then says, "Butch Kane."

The priest smiles. "I thought you might remember me. But my name isn't really Butch. It's Leonard. Lenny's what I go by now. That, and Father Kane."

"Why'd everyone in school call you Butch?"

"I made them call me that. I thought it made me sound tough."

"You were tough," Remi says. Then, "What do you remember about me?"

"You had the reputation of being a good fighter. But when I came for you, it didn't take but a couple good punches to put you down, and I thought you were a waste of time. Then, a year later, I sought you out again, and this time, you gave me a run for my money. I still put you down, but it was more work."

"I remember. It was pretty close between us that second time."

"You'd been practicing."

Remi nods. He tells the tale of how, when he turned fifteen, his old man decided it was time to beat on him. "At first, I figured he was trying to toughen me up. Trying to be a good dad, make up for being such a shitty husband to my mother. But after a while I came to see it for what it was—just him beating on me because it was fun."

Remi explains that he'd go to school with black eyes and swollen lips, too embarrassed to say it was his own father who'd done it to him. So he made up stories that he'd gotten into fights with kids at other schools. Big kids, sometimes more than one. "You should see what *they* look like," he'd tell his classmates.

"It didn't take long for the tough kids in our school to come looking for me, try me out, prove themselves. Guys like you."

The priest nods. "Guys like me."

"At first, I got the shit kicked out of me. But in time, I learned how to throw a punch, and avoid one. Learned where to hit someone to take away their breath. By the time I was sixteen, I came to be a good fighter. By the time I was seventeen, I came to like it. That became a problem."

Lenny Kane refills his glass. Takes a sip. He studies Remi for a minute. "So, how did things end with your father?"

Remi looks at his glass but doesn't give in. "Year after I graduated, we came to an understanding," he says, seeing himself at nineteen, finally having had enough of the beatings, standing over the old man, lying on the living room floor, his nose broken, mouth bleeding, eyes already swelling shut. The wicked bastard looking up at him, laughing, saying, "Finally! I knew it. I knew you had the violence in you. Seems you're my son, after all." Seeing himself turn away in disgust, at himself as much as his father, vowing an end to the fighting.

"I heard you had some trouble after graduation," the priest says. "Was that before or after you went overseas?"

"Both. Before I served, I fell in with a bad crowd, did some stupid stuff, small stuff. After I came back, I fell in with a worse crowd, pulled some real stunts. Went upstate, things just got worse."

"How old were you when you joined the war?"

"Was twenty-three. Part of Desert Shield, the buildup to the fighting. Then Desert Storm."

"How was that, for you?"

Remi opens his hands. "Did what had to be done, same as everybody. You were there too, I heard."

"First Marine Expeditionary Force."

"Going by Butch or Lenny, then?"

"Still Butch. Still the tough guy. Why I joined the Marines in the first place."

The priest takes another swallow, then gets down to business. "So, why are we here?"

Remi tells the priest about Kayla and his need to pay for her Ivy League education, then passes on what he'd been told by the cardiologist.

"Chuckie Paxton." Lenny Kane repeats the name, and smiles. "Mouthy little shit. I used to smack him around once or twice a year just to keep him in line."

The two men sit quietly for a moment, the priest sipping his Johnny Walker, Remi looking at the second glass.

"So, how can I help you with your problem? If you don't know from the media, you should be able to tell by looking around that our parish isn't in a position to help you financially."

"No. I can get the money myself. The problem is *how* I can get it."

Father Kane leans forward. "Please tell me you're not planning on doing something stupid."

"Worse than stupid."

The priest looks at Remi, then, "Just how far up the sin chain are we talking here?"

Remi reaches for the whiskey, throws it back. Tells the priest about the drug dealer peddling heroin to high-school kids, about what he's going to do to the guy.

When he's done talking, Father Kane says, "I was going to ask you why you came to me given that you're not a member of this parish, or even a Catholic for that matter, but now I'm guessing you couldn't bring yourself to share this type of thing with your reverend. Do I have it right?"

"Close enough."

"That stuff about the guy being a dealer, you think that makes a difference?"

"One of the things I want to know. Does it?"

The priest hesitates. "No."

"You don't seem so sure."

"Is that how you're reading me? What you expected from me? That since I used to be a tough guy like you, because I went overseas and did what had to be done, I'd give you the green light on this? A wink and a nod and say a few prayers and don't worry, God will forgive you because the guy's a bad actor?"

Remi doesn't answer.

"That's not how it works, Bone, even when it comes to killing one of the bad guys. And not even a former hard case like me will tell you otherwise."

Remi takes a sip, looks away, then back at the priest.

"There's a story in John about Jesus curing a blind man. He bends down, spits in the dirt, makes some mud and puts it onto the blind guy's eyes and he can see again."

"Okay."

"Point is, we got to give him something to work with. To make the blind see, it took some mud."

Remi stares.

"When it's forgiveness you're looking for, that something is remorse."

"But I am sorry for what I might do."

"Remorse is a lot stronger than sorry. Remorse is once you've done something, you're so upset it eats away at you, so disturbed you can't sleep or eat, so tormented you'd give anything to go back in time and not do it. Your 'sorry' is you feel a little bad but you're going to do it anyway. That's not sorry, Bone. It's bullshit."

Remi looks down.

Lenny Kane pauses for a moment, switches gears. "How'd a guy like you end up a father and a husband?"

Remi thinks on this a minute. "Guess I just found something I didn't know I was looking for. How'd you end up a priest?"

The big man doesn't answer, but his eyes get a faraway look that tells Remi it was much the same for Butch Kane.

"You can't do it, Remi, what you're thinking. There's no way back from that kind of thing."

"Wouldn't be the first time I took a life."

"You were a soldier, same as me. It's different."

Remi looks away, not thinking about his stint overseas, but seeing himself being beaten by a lifer in the prison yard one day, seeing himself standing over the same lifer a week later, the man bleeding out from a slashed carotid artery. Twenty guys standing around watching and not one ratted him out to the guards.

"Oh, I see."

"Was a self-preservation kind of thing."

"Nothing stronger, I suppose."

"One thing is stronger," Remi says, thinking of Kayla.

"You won't be helping her, Bone. What she needs is to remember her father as a good man. An Ivy League education won't make up for a dad who's a murderer."

"So I best not get caught."

The priest pauses. "I'm starting to think maybe it's time for me to call up old Butch. Take you out back, beat some sense into you."

Remi nods to his glass and the priest pours them both another drink.

"What are you thinking?" asks the priest.

"I'm thinking it's been so long since I've had a real drink, I forgot how good it is."

"So, on top of it all, you're going to start back down that path, too. I'm not feeling like a very good priest right now."

"Go easy on yourself. Even Jesus needed something to work with. What you told me."

CHAPTER THIRTEEN

"PIGGY MANAGES TO get his fat ass up onto that truck, I'll flap my arms and fly away." Rizzo snorts and sips some coffee from the paper cup. He and Flynn are sitting in their unmarked sedan, on 5th Street, just off West Sedgley, in front of the Pentecostal church. A beat-up truck trailer covered with graffiti is parked in a lot across the street, and they got a tip it's where Piggy Rodriguez keeps his stash of cannabis, the snitch also telling Rizzo that Piggy is coming that afternoon to pick up a suitcase full.

"What do you think he goes?" says Flynn. "Three hundred?"

"Try three-fifty, at least."

"He should sign up for the Wing Bowl," Flynn says, referring to the annual eating competition, held before 20,000 fans at the Wells Fargo Center before it was canceled.

"You'd think those guys'd be huge, but they're not. Notorious Bob, Dave Brunelli, they're big guys, but nothing like Piggy."

"I shouldn't'a mentioned the Wing Bowl; now I got to take a dump."

Rizzo's iPhone rings. He lifts it from his pocket, his blood pressure spiking as soon as he sees the number. After a moment, he answers. "Yeah," he says.

"Ed, it's Marie at Sunset Senior Living."

"What now?"

"Leeza really did it this time."

"Just tell me."

"There was a dust-up at bingo. Apparently, Sarah Cranford took your mother's seat. There was a lot of yelling, then Leeza started in with the threats."

"That's no big deal—she always makes threats."

"Well, this time, she acted."

Rizzo closes his eyes. "What'd she do?"

"She removed her Depends, walked into Mrs. Cranford's room, and urinated on her couch."

Rizzo exhales. "I'll be there."

"We can't have this sort of thing—"

"Unbelievable," Rizzo says, hanging up.

"What?"

"Take me back to the station. I have to pick up my car and drive to the old folks home, see my mother."

"It's called *assisted living* now, not old folks home. You're not PC."

"You ever go to one, you'll call it an old folks home, too. Bunch of white-hairs sitting around in wheelchairs. They herd them into the big room for Karaoke night, looks like a goddamn box of Q-tips."

*   *   *

An hour later, Rizzo walks into Sunset Senior Living on Baltimore Pike. He sees the sign and his mind skips to the brochures showing old people sitting around a table, laughing, carrying on, above a banner that reads, "Don't bother visiting this weekend, son, I'm way too busy!"

"What a crock."

The facility is housed in an old stone mansion that was home to a department store magnate a hundred years before. It's the latest stop in what Rizzo thinks of as his mother's farewell tour, "Leeza" Rizzo having been kicked out of three other homes before Sunset.

Rizzo enters the lobby and pauses to steel himself. No one is on the direct-from-grandmother's-house Queen Anne chairs or sofa, but four or five women are parked on wheelchairs around the room. Two of them are speaking to each other, two more stare into space, and one looks to be asleep, her neck almost horizontal to her torso.

Rizzo crosses the worn carpet, past the unused billiard room and the empty library to the elevator. Riding to the second floor, he scans the events listed for the month: Fitness Fun every morning, bingo in the afternoons, karaoke night, movie night, ice-cream social, Beading with Betty, Brainteasers with Bob. His mother has made herself the star of each of them, with the exception of movie night, which she boycotts because, "they never show anything hot."

When Rizzo enters her room, he finds his mother standing by her walker, tapping on her cellphone. She looks up at him and smiles, until she sees the look on his face. "What?"

"Don't pretend you don't know why I'm here."

"I know why you should be here: because I'm your mother, and you miss me. It's not like you don't have time since that evil wife of yours ran off."

"That was fifteen years ago, Mom. And Sally left me because I was a drunk and a run-around," he says, remembering it all coming to a head the night he arrived home to find all of his clothes on the lawn, and him waking up the next morning in the back of his police cruiser, naked, with that hot redhead patrol officer.

"And when's the last time you heard from your daughter? *Elizabeth*. The big scientist just had to move to California, three-thousand miles away."

"She calls me every day to remind me I won father-of-the-year."

"Yeah, stick up for her. You're too forgiving."

Rizzo shakes his head. "What were you thinking, Mom? Urinating on her couch?"

"She has no respect. And it was an accident."

"An accident? You took off your diaper before you did it."

"It's an undergarment. What am I, two years old?"

"You're worse than a two-year-old."

"This place sucks. It's even worse than the others."

"It's the only place that would take you. The only place left." Rizzo sits down and motions for his mother to do the same.

"I don't like sitting," she says, but does it anyway.

"Mom, please listen to me. I practically had to beg to get you in here. They found out about you being kicked out of those other places."

"Ha! They had an empty room, is all it took."

"You're running out of assisted living homes to—"

"Assisted dying, you mean."

Rizzo takes a deep breath, counts to five.

"You know where I got the idea? *Seinfeld*. Remember that episode where Poppie pees on Jerry's new couch?"

"Jesus, Mom."

"Call me Leeza."

"I'm not calling you *Leeza*. That's not even your name."

"Do you have your car or your truck?"

"The car. Why?"

"I can't get in the truck; it's too high. And we need to go see Father Kane."

"You'll see him on Sunday."

"I'm not waiting. I have a venal sin on my soul, thanks to that bitch Sarah Cranford, and I have to give my confession."

"You just want to flirt with that priest."

Leeza smiles. "He looks like your father. And I haven't had any companionship since Earl Moody."

"The hell is Earl Moody?"

"My latest bed-warmer. He passed, two weeks ago."

"For crying out loud, Mom. I don't need to hear this."

"Come on," she says, standing and grabbing for the walker.

When they arrive at the church, he pulls her walker from the back seat and helps her out of the car. The walker gets caught on the lip at the bottom of the concrete handicap ramp, and Leeza starts to fall forward but is caught by a thin man with large hands who appears to Rizzo to be in his fifties.

Rizzo thanks the man, who tells him to think nothing of it, something about him, or his voice, seeming familiar to Rizzo. Turning to watch the man go, Rizzo tries to remember where he'd seen him, but he can't.

"Hello, Father!" Leeza sings to the priest, who's appeared in the doorway.

Leeza thanks Father Kane for greeting them at the door, but Rizzo can tell by where he's looking that it's not for them he's standing there. Rizzo glances back and sees the thin man climb into an F-150.

Looking back at the priest, he sees distress in his eyes.

"That guy give you trouble, Father?" Rizzo says. Then, smiling, "He someone I need to arrest?"

But the priest doesn't smile back.

CHAPTER FOURTEEN

PULLING OUT OF the church lot, Remi glances at the man and the old woman standing with the priest. He knows the man from somewhere, but he doesn't know where. He could probably have placed him if he'd stayed and talked a few minutes, but he needs to pick up Kayla. And he wanted to put some distance between himself and Butch Kane. He'd gone to see the priest hoping for something, he didn't know what, but whatever it was, he didn't find it.

He wipes his brow, sweaty from the booze. Only a few swallows, but enough to give him a little buzz, him not having tasted hard liquor in a decade. That was part of his deal with Bea. No booze. So he made the promise, and stuck to it, even after Bea's passing.

He thinks again about the priest, wondering what had transformed Butch Kane into Father Lenny. With him, all it had taken was a chance encounter on the road. On his way to a grand old time and got himself struck by lightning. Though not the type of strike to light a man up, but to quiet him.

He pulls up to the high school and Kayla jumps in the truck, talking at a hundred miles an hour even before she shuts the door. This one said that, the other one did this, those two did such-and-such. The tone of her voice hopscotching from "what an idiot" to "isn't that the funniest thing you ever heard?" to "I feel so sad for her." The speed making it impossible to follow, the teenager content making it impossible to understand, being alien to him, a man in his fifties.

Then, all of a sudden, nothing, just Kayla staring out the windshield, her lips pursed. He's used to the moodiness, the sudden squalls coming out of nowhere. Hormones, and all that. He's learned the best strategy is to keep quiet, let it pass. Duck and cover.

They arrive home, and he warms some leftover meatloaf, Kayla setting the table, still not talking. Just glaring at him every now and then. They eat in silence, him figuring out it's him she's upset with but not knowing why. When they're finished, she helps him load the dishwasher, taking turns rinsing off the plates and silverware first.

She turns to him, her arms crossed, fire in her eyes. "I know what booze smells like, Remi. And don't tell me it was beer because it wasn't."

So that's it.

"You want to tell me what's going on?"

"I just got together with an old friend is all. We shared a drink."

"What old friend is that?"

"Butch Kane, guy I went to school with."

"How come I never heard of him?"

"No reason for me to mention him. I haven't seen him in years. I only just ran into him. He's a priest now, over at Holy Redeemer."

She narrows her eyes, studies him.

"What are you doing drinking booze with some priest in the afternoon?"

"We was talking. The booze just showed up."

"So, you ran into an old priest friend and you felt you needed to talk to him. What's going on?"

He sighs. "I'm just feeling a little stress is all. Nothing to worry about."

Her eyes fill. "I know what's happening. I knew all along. There's no way we can afford me going to Penn—"

"That's not it at all—"

"It's a pipe dream."

It's his turn to get angry. "Now, you listen to me. You're going to that school. You have the brains, and you earned it."

"It costs fifty thousand dollars a year. I looked it up. That's crazy money. Way more than we have."

"There's money left over from your mother's life insurance. And I've been saving. Deke's always pressing me to work more, and once you're at school, I'll have extra time to take him up on it."

She stares at him and he reads both hope and doubt in her eyes. He reaches forward, grabs her shoulders. "You're going to be an Ivy League girl, and I'm going to pay for it, whatever it takes."

She hesitates, then reaches around and hugs him.

And there it is.

He hugs her back, then releases her to her room and her iPhone. As soon as he hears her shut the door, he gets his own cellphone and makes the call.

"Deke. Bone. I'm ready now. Let's get this done."

*   *   *

Kayla sits on her bed, but there's no talking, texting, or tweeting going on. Instead, she mentally reviews her conversation with Remi. He's hiding something, and she knows it. She hasn't smelled liquor on his breath since the day she met him. That was eleven years earlier, her mother driving her to the King of Prussia mall, their car breaking down on the Schuylkill expressway and a stranger stopping to help. The man pulled ahead of them in a pickup truck, walked back, offered to look under the hood. He spent some time then told her mother she was going to need a tow; meantime, he'd drive them to the garage he worked at, some-place along Lancaster Avenue in the western burbs. Her mother wouldn't let him take them any place until he showed her his driv-er's license.

"Remington Bone?" she asked.

"Last name's pronounced 'Bo-Nay,' but most people read the 'H' as silent and say 'Bone,' like you. I go by Remi. Or Bone."

"I'd rather wait for Triple-A," her mother had said, "but I don't like sitting on the highway with my daughter in the car."

So she agreed to let him drive them while the car was towed to his garage. There was no place for them to sit so he drove them to the local library. A couple hours later, he showed up with their car, "purring like a kitten, but you need a new back right tire."

He said he'd charge them only for the parts, but her mother insisted on paying something toward the labor. "I earn my money and I don't take charity," she'd said.

"He seemed nice," Kayla had told her mother after they left the garage, having dropped Remi off.

"They all seem nice at first." The words cynical, but her mother smiling.

That was the beginning of it, between Remi and her mother. The end of it, of course, came with her mother's cancer. "Now, I want you to listen to what I'm going to tell you,"— her mother saying one night on her deathbed when the two of them were alone. "Remi's a good man. But he's the kind that can be swayed down the wrong path. He's going to need you to watch over him.

But he can't ever see it that way. He has to think it's him watching over you. Your need to be protected is the only thing that'll keep him on the straight and narrow."

That was her first real lesson on how men's minds work. She took it to heart, making sure Remi Bone never forgot how much she needed him, starting with her little performance at the gravesite.

She was also careful to watch him for signs of slippage, the most important of which was evidence of drinking. Her mother had been fine with Remi having a beer or two after work, a little more on weekends. She planned to toe the same line, but it never became an issue—Remi never drinking liquor in her presence or coming home with the smell of it on his breath.

Until today. Yes, something was most definitely up, and if she saw any more signs, she'd look into it herself. Maybe go see that priest, the supposed old friend who appeared out of nowhere. Or talk to Remi's boss, Deke, though he creeped her out.

She reaches over to the nightstand, lifts the picture frame. Her, Remi, and her mom, a couple of years before her mom passed. Everyone smiling, having no idea what was in store for them.

CHAPTER FIFTEEN

REMI TAKES HIS time finishing with his last car. He moves more slowly than normal as he cleans up his workspace and washes his hands. Eventually, though, there's nothing for him to do other than talk to Deke. He exhales, walks toward Deke's office. His eyes on Deke the whole way, he enters, closes the door, and sits in front of the desk.

"So, you're really ready to do this?" asks Deke.

"I'm ready."

"You sure, because—"

"Just get to it."

"Not a man to beat around the bush. I respect that."

Remi stares.

"Okay, then," Deke says. "Here's how it's going to go down. A guy's going to come to the garage about midnight tomorrow, pick you up in a car. Guy's name is Virgil. Car is going to be a Subaru Legacy. Blue. He's going to take you up to the Badlands, drive you around, to a bar called the 'No-Name,' because it's got no name. Sign outside is just a black piece of wood.

"Around one a.m., Castillo—this is him—" he says, sliding a picture across his desk— "is going to get a call telling him to go to a building close by, something's up. He's going to leave the bar out the back door, going to walk through the backyard to an alley. On the other side of the alley is another yard that belongs to the other building. You're going to be in that alley. You're going to shoot Castillo. Once in the heart to put him down. Once in the head to make sure the job's done.

"Then, you're going to walk to the end of the alley and Virgil's going to pick you up, bring you back to the garage."

Remi thinks for a minute. "What am I going use? To shoot him with?"

Deke smiles, reaches into the bottom desk drawer, and lifts out a metal box. He unlocks it with a key from his pocket, opens the lid, and removes something wrapped in cloth. Deke slides the object across the desk, toward Remi.

"Unwrap it."

Remi does so and sees the gun.

"It's a .38 special. A revolver. Six shells."

"Looks old."

"It is. But it works. And it's untraceable."

Remi stares at the weapon. This is no longer just two guys talking about something. Imagining it. Bullshitting. It's two guys about to *do it*.

Deke takes back the gun, replaces it into the box. "Virgil's going to have the gun in the car. That way you don't have to carry it around. When you're done and you're in the car again, give the gun back to him. You got all that?"

"Let's talk about the money."

"Like I told you the other day, guy's offering ten thousand. I figure we split it fifty-fifty."

"No. And no. You tell me it's ten thousand, I'm guessing it's twenty-five. And I want more than half, way more, since I'm the one pulling the trigger."

Deke leans back in his seat. "He offered me ten, and that's the truth. I could maybe get him to twenty, but I'd still want half, as the one putting this all together."

"Stop bullshitting me, Deke. He'll offer twenty-five, if he hasn't already. I'll take twenty. You keep the five. You want me to do it, that's what it has to be."

Deke's face is red, and Remi sees him fighting to hold his temper. "I'll make a call, is all I can do. But don't hold your breath."

Remi nods toward the phone. "Make the call, then."

"With you listening in?"

Remi stands, knowing Deke isn't going to make a call, doesn't have to. "Come get me when you're done." He goes to the cluttered locker room and waits. It doesn't take long.

"I can't believe it, but he came up to twenty-five. Wasn't easy convincing him, though." Deke shakes his head, walking and talking. He stops two feet from where Remi's standing and they face off, until Deke says, "You can't mess this up."

Remi's face is stone.

"You hear me? You can't fuck this up. You think you're going to fuck it up, tell me now."

"Just get the money. Twenty thousand."

With that, Remi turns and leaves.

CHAPTER SIXTEEN

JUST BEFORE MIDNIGHT. Remi stands behind the iron gate connecting the concrete walls enclosing the parking lot of Buford's Garage. A dark blue Subaru Legacy pulls up beyond the walls, and Remi unlatches the gate, walks across the sidewalk, and leans through the open passenger door window. He's surprised by the driver. Given the business at hand, he expected to be picked up by some dirtbag in worn army fatigues and jeans. An old hard case. A drunk with greasy hair. But the driver is young. His short blond hair looks like it was just cut. And he's wearing a sweater vest, of all things.

"You Virgil?"

"Yes, sir." The young man smiles. Perfect rows of white teeth.

Remi gets in and they pull away.

It takes thirty minutes to reach the Kensington section of the city. Remi uses the time to take the revolver from the glove compartment and look at it. He pops the release to open the cylinder. Six chambers, six bullets. He closes the cylinder and inspects the rest of the gun: the trigger, guard, hammer, barrel and front sight, ejector rod.

"Check out okay?" asks Virgil. Trying to make small talk.

"When's the last time this was cleaned and oiled?"

"Gee, I don't know anything about that gun, or any guns. I've never even fired one."

"I don't want this thing jamming on me."

Virgil doesn't answer, keeping his eyes on the road.

Remi looks the gun over some more, then puts it into the large side pocket of his coat.

"What kinda name is Virgil?"

"I think it's originally Italian, sir. But my family's Mormon. My first name is Dallen but everyone calls me by my middle name, because I have, like, four cousins named Dallen."

"You pulling my leg? I thought the Mormons were all out in Utah." As soon as Remi says it, he remembers the big temple the Mormons had completed in Center City some years before.

"Oh, no. I'm from Utah, originally. But we're all over. Forty thousand right here in Philadelphia. Although I shouldn't say *we* since I got kicked out."

"Kicked out, huh? What'd you do?"

Virgil's shoulders slump a bit. "I'd rather not say, sir."

They sit quietly for a while, then Remi notices the GPS screen to the right of the steering wheel. "What's that for?"

"Uber X. I'm a driver."

"You're shitting me. You driving me's an Uber thing?"

"Oh, goodness no. I'm off the clock. When we're done, I'll log in, start making money."

"No one's tracking this car, right? I mean, the Uber people."

"Not when I'm off duty. They don't know where I am."

Remi gives Virgil a hard look, then turns and watches the road ahead.

"This what they call the Badlands?"

"We're right in the heart of it."

"Where's that El Campamento?" asks Remi, referring to the notorious, trash-strewn gorge reputed to be home to a hundred heroin addicts. He'd read an article in the *Inquirer* calling it a "Heroin Hellscape." According to the paper, the ground is littered with half a million used syringes, and many cops won't enter it for fear of pricking themselves.

"Not far. Down by the tracks. Between 2nd to the north and the Market-Frankford El to the south. Separates Kensington from the Fairhill section."

"You ever been down there?"

"That's a dangerous place. And supposedly very dirty."

"Dirty, huh?" Remi studies the young driver, wondering what the kid had done to be run out of his church, and how he'd ended up driving someone to a hit.

"That's the bar," says Virgil.

Ahead on the right, Remi sees a run-down brick building with a black sign out front.

"As soon as I turn the corner, you can look out your window, see the bar's backyard and the alley. When it's time, someone's going to call me, tell me to drop you off on the other end of the alley. Then you go down the alley to the backyard of the bar and wait. The guy you're looking for will come out shortly."

"Mind if I ask who's going to be calling you?"

"I'm not supposed to tell you that."

Remi looks at his watch. He has another twenty, twenty-five minutes until Castillo is supposed to leave the bar. "Take me to the drug camp," he says.

"I don't think that's a very good idea, sir."

"I want to see it for myself."

Virgil shakes his head, but drives to East Tusculum Street, near Front, and stops.

"Be careful," Virgil says. "There's needles everywhere. And dead bodies. "When someone ODs, the other addicts just hide them, so the police won't come."

Remi leaves the car and carefully walks down an embankment into a lightly wooded area. It's dark but the moon gives him enough light to see. When he gets to the bottom, he looks around. Every square inch of ground is covered by debris—bottles, cans, paper, discarded clothing, tires, broken pieces of furniture. And everywhere, used syringes. Thousands upon thousands of them.

Ahead on the ground, and on the embankment, Remi sees what appear to be small piles of winter clothing. He approaches one and sees a hand protruding from the arm of a jacket. *Jesus.* Carefully, he leans down and rolls the body over. He forces himself to look at the face and jumps back when sees that the eyes are looking up at him. *This isn't a body, it's a person.*

Remi catches his breath, then says, "Hey, are you okay?"

But the man doesn't answer. Doesn't move. Just keeps staring with a strange faraway look on his face. Remi realizes then that the man isn't looking at him at all. Probably doesn't even see him.

Remi steps back and looks around. He can see at least two dozen addicts lying motionless in the dirt and trash. The newspaper was right: this really is a scene right out of hell.

About twenty feet away is what appears to be a shack made out of plywood and wood pallets, and he walks up to it. A curtain of cloth hangs over one corner and Remi pushes it aside. Sitting against the far wall are a pair of heroin zombies staring into space. Lying on the floor by their feet is a third. But this one, Remi can tell for sure, is dead.

He stumbles out of the shack, falls to his knees, and throws up. When he's finished, he climbs the embankment, spots the blue Subaru, and gets in.

"You look like you've seen a ghost," Virgil says.

Staring through the windshield, Remi nods. "A whole bunch of 'em. Most still alive."

Virgil hands him a bottle of Ethos water. "Here, drink this. It has electrolytes, and they donate money so kids in third-world countries will have adequate drinking water. From your breath, I can tell you need some."

Remi swishes some of the water around in his mouth and spits it through the open window. Does it again. "Let's go," he says and Virgil starts the car and drives them away.

A minute later, Virgil's phone rings. He answers, says a few words, then hangs up. "This is it. Are you ready?"

Ready to kill a heroin dealer? After what I saw? "Damn right I am."

Virgil deposits Remi at the end of the alley. It's a gravel and dirt pathway bordered on both sides by tall scraggly hedges. Remi walks down to the yard behind the bar and crouches in wait for Castillo. He lets his breath catch up with him, then quietly practices his line: "The righteous will rejoice when he sees the vengeance; he will bathe his feet in the blood of the wicked."

He says it over and over until Remi Bone starts to fade away, his body taken over by Samuel L. Jackson as Jules Winnfield. Doubt is replaced by confidence. Shaky nerves by steel.

He waits, crouched, ready to spring. Ready to bring vengeance to the heroin dealer who turns people into zombies. Turns *kids* into corpses.

He waits. And he waits. His legs start to burn, so he stands. But that's no good because someone approaching could see his head above the hedges. So he gets down on one knee. Until it starts to hurt and he switches knees.

Twenty minutes have passed and Castillo hasn't shown. Jackson and Winnfield are long gone now. Remi is alone. And he's starting to feel nervous. His bum ticker is pounding hard in his chest and he's wondering whether it will give out before Castillo arrives. That would be an awful thing. The drug dealer would see him lying there, look him over, maybe see what he has in his pockets. Take the gun and the cash from his wallet then leave him there, until the smell got bad enough that someone alerted the police. Sooner or later, a detective would come to his house and tell Kayla—by then frantic with worry—that her father was dead. Question her about what he was doing up in the Badlands. Her life would come crashing down on her and she'd spend the rest of it wondering what he *was* doing there. Wondering who was he, after all, this Remi Bone who'd married her mother and promised to take care of her when her mother died.

"Who the hell are you?"

Remi shoots to his feet and pulls out the pistol. He recognizes Castillo from the photo Deke showed him. He'd been so lost in his thoughts, he hadn't heard the criminal leave the bar and walk across the yard, or push through the hedges into the alley.

His gun pointed at Castillo, he searches his mind for the words. The magic words of vengeance that will transform him back into the cool professional hit man. But what comes out, as he stands there pointing the gun with his right hand and holding his pounding chest with his left, aren't the divinely inspired words from Psalm 58, but something else entirely:

"Tick tock, says the clock. Time's up, motherfuck."

Castillo steps back and closes his eyes, and Remi sees that he knows what's coming. Except it doesn't come because Remi freezes.

Castillo opens his left eye, then his right, and the two men face off. Remi can see that Castillo is studying him, appraising him.

After a minute, the drug dealer fashions his look into one of sympathy. "You don't want to do this, I can tell. You're a good person."

Remi hears the words, sees the concern in Castillo's eyes. He also sees the man slowly reach behind his back as he continues talking in a smooth, sympathetic tone. Sees his arm start moving forward again, first slow then fast. Sees the glint of metal.

He pulls the trigger. The other man's eyes widen, as he's pushed back a step. Widen in surprise, then fear, then anger.

Castillo's knees buckle and he crumbles straight to the ground in a heap. The gun is still in his hand.

Remi sees the blood pumping out of Castillo's chest, bubbling up out of his mouth. There's something he's supposed to do now, but he can't remember what it is. He puts the gun back into his coat pocket and walks past Castillo, crouches down in the shadows so no one can see him. Waits for the Subaru to pull up at the end of the alley, now only about ten feet away.

But the car doesn't show. He waits until he can't bear it, then waits some more. Then, from behind him, he senses movement, and he freezes. He hears something making its way along the gravel. Hears footsteps, and breathing. He stops breathing himself, and forces himself to turn around, remembering what he was supposed to do after he shot Castillo in the heart: shoot him again, in the head, to make sure.

He sees the eyes looking at him even before he's done turning. Dark eyes, bright with intelligence. Evaluating him. But not the eyes of Castillo, who lays where he fell. Instead, the eyes that study him belong to a dog. A black pit bull, with a white star on its chest. The dog walks up to Castillo, sniffs him. Then, satisfied—or so it seems to Remi—he lifts his leg and urinates on Castillo's face.

When the dog is finished, he lowers his leg, and walks down the alley, pausing once to look back at Remi before moving on.

Remi clutches his chest and feels like crying. The star-chested dog was a sign. A sign if ever there was one. God approved of what he'd done to the wicked heroin pusher.

Just then Remi hears the car pull up by the alley. He gets up, half runs, half stumbles his way to the Subaru. "Where the hell were you?" he grumbles as Virgil pulls away. "Seemed like I was waiting there forever."

"Gee, I'm really sorry, sir. After I dropped you off, I got a call that your guy wasn't going to be leaving for, like, an hour. So—"

"Why didn't you come and pick me up? Instead of making me wait in that alley not knowing what was going on?"

"I would've come and gotten you, for sure," Virgil says. "If he'd have told me. But he said to just drive around."

"Why didn't your boss, or whoever is calling the shots for you, call me on my cell and tell me?"

"I don't know. Does he have your number?"

"What a clusterfuck. You know the guy had the jump on me? If he'd known why I was there, he'd have shot me dead. He almost did anyway."

"Wow, that's awful. I'm really sorry that happened."

"And you just drove around all this time?"

"Well . . ."

Remi sees Virgil glance at his GPS. "Are you kidding me? You went Ubering while I was in that alley?"

"I stayed close. I was only a mile away, at the farthest."

"This is unbelievable." Remi thinks for a minute. "Who takes Uber in this neighborhood?"

Virgil explains it was a young guy in black leather pants with two provocatively dressed women. He picked them up at a bar and dropped them off at a motel.

Remi shakes his head. He's still breathing hard and is drenched with sweat. "Just take me back to the garage."

Forty minutes later they pull up outside of Buford's. As they come to a stop, Virgil says, "It was great working with you, sir. Seeing as how you made it back to the car, I guess everything worked out okay. I mean, your boss and my boss are going to be happy, right?"

Remi has one foot out the door but he turns and stares at the kid, all smiling and perky. He shakes his head. *It's like I'm sitting next to Donny Osmond from hell.* "I think you should just stick to the Uber thing, son. Leave this nasty business behind."

"That would be great, if I could. But, well. I have obligations. You know, debts that have to be . . ."

The kid still talking, Remi closes the door and leaves him.

CHAPTER SEVENTEEN

REMI IS THREE STEPS into the house when Kayla confronts him. "Do you know what time it is? Where have you been?"

"I was at the garage. I told you I was going to be late, had a special car had to be fixed by morning."

"Let me smell your breath."

"My breath?"

She leans in, makes him blow. "Oh, man. Did you throw up?"

"Just a little. I think I might have a bug."

Kayla puts her hand on his forehead. "You don't have a fever. You're not sweating, or pale. It wasn't a bug that made you puke."

They stand facing each other, her with her hands on her hips, him with his shoulders stooped, wondering just when Beatrice had reincarnated herself as Kayla.

"This isn't like you, Remi. Something's going on. And I want to know what it is, right now."

"Now hold on, just one minute. Who's the parent here, and who's the child?"

"I'm beginning to wonder."

"I've had enough of your cross-examining. You go on up to bed. And don't be questioning me no more."

Kayla crosses her arms, stares at him for a long while, then turns and stomps up the steps. At the top, she calls down. "And when is my car going to be fixed? It's been a week. I'm tired of having to be driven everywhere."

"I'll have it back to you tomorrow."

She glares at him, then turns away.

His heart pounding, he waits for her to disappear into her room, then exhales. In the kitchen, with the light off, he sits down at the table, folds his hands in front of him, stays that way for a long time, staring into the blackness. It's so quiet he hears the second hand of his wristwatch ticking away.

"Tick tock says the clock." *Jesus.*

His head grows heavier on his neck, starts a slow wobble that makes him feel faint. That and his breathing, which grows shallower and quieter. He wonders whether his heart, his bum ticker, his piece of junk, will just stop beating.

It doesn't, and after minutes that pass like hours, he pushes himself from the chair and wills himself up the steps to the bathroom. He stands before the medicine cabinet mirror.

The face is the same, the man behind it, different. No longer just a killer for country, and self-preservation, but the type that stalks another man, hunts him down, like prey. For money. He feels an emptiness, a diminishment of himself. He is smaller now than he was before. Less.

He turns, doubles over the toilet, and vomits.

Eventually, he becomes aware of another presence. He looks behind him, sees Kayla, concern in her eyes, and the other thing, anger, both wrapped by the thing that scares him the most, determination.

CHAPTER EIGHTEEN

RIZZO THROWS BACK the cup, takes a big gulp of strong, black coffee. "Boy, that's good." Eighteen inches from the tips of Rizzo's shoes is the body of Rolli Castillo. The CSU team having already taken their pictures and measurements, Rizzo and Flynn are free to examine the scene before the corpse is hauled away.

"This is just wonderful," says Bart Carlton, the assistant district attorney, on the other side of the body. "I could kick this idiot." He lifts his foot but holds himself back, not wanting to give some slimy defense attorney ammunition to argue that he tampered with the crime scene.

"Looks like someone was lying in wait for him," Rizzo says, taking in the footprints on the ground, the knee prints. "They knew he was going to leave the bar, cross the alley. Maybe not so certain as to when," he adds, the markings telling him the killer was waiting for a while, trying to get comfortable.

"So this was a hit?" asks Flynn.

"What else?" says Carlton.

"What's on his face?" Flynn leans down for a closer look. "Jeez, it smells like urine. You think the killer pissed on him?"

"Not the killer," says Rizzo, noticing the paw prints in the wet earth, thinking of the little black dog that had been prowling the neighborhood for years, tough little bastard he once saw hit by a car and when the driver stopped to help him, he pissed on the guy's shoe and limped away.

"He must've had nerves of steel," Flynn says. "Bullet looks like it went straight through the heart, the guy confident enough in his shot he knew he didn't need a second. Probably a pro."

"Plus, look at that," Rizzo says, nodding to the pistol in the dead man's right hand. "Rolli was pulling out his gun. The killer would've seen that. But he didn't panic, kept his weapon pointed straight at the heart, then fired."

"Just wonderful," Carlton repeats, glaring at Rizzo like it's all his fault.

"Don't even think about putting this on me. I told him he shouldn't'a been walking around. Should've gone into protective custody."

"Well, so did I," the ADA says, getting defensive. "But he was too smart to listen. Well *how smart do you feel now?*" He leans into the corpse, wanting more than anything to stomp it in the face.

"What do you think Rolli was doing out here?" asks Flynn, his inexperience causing him to lose sight of the key issue: who in law enforcement was going to get blamed for the screwup.

Rizzo and the attorney stare at each other, until Rizzo, looking toward the back door of the No-Name, says, "Well, if that's point A, and he was walking in a straight line, then Point B would have to be . . . that building right there." With that, he pushes his way through the hedges into the backyard of the building across the alley from the bar. Flynn follows him and they both pull their weapons as they approach the dilapidated red brick structure. Carlton stays behind pretending to answer a call on his cellphone.

Rizzo moves up to the building's back door and, after a few kicks, shouts back to Flynn, loud enough for the ADA to hear,

"Look, it's unlocked, and open. Let's peek our heads inside, see what's in plain view."

They enter and find a large open room, empty except for some folding tables covered with aluminum foil squares, empty wax and plastic bags, vials, and tape dispensers. Most of the bags are small, but there are some larger Ziploc bags, too.

"No cook's lab," Rizzo says. "So this was just a place for packaging."

"But you were right about him still being in the business," says Flynn. "So when was this place cleaned out—and by who?"

"Last night. By whoever helped set Rolli up for the hit."

Rizzo leads Flynn back to the body and ADA Carlton. "Let's roll. There's nothing more to do here," Rizzo says.

"Shouldn't we go into the bar?" says Flynn. "See if anyone will tell us anything?"

Carlton rolls his eyes, looks at Rizzo. "Just how green is this guy?"

Rizzo ignores him, leads Flynn back to the car. "No one at that bar is going to remember anything," he tells his young partner. "And you can be certain every one of those six guys Rolli ratted on will pretend they never heard his name before. The only possible break in this case will be if ballistics can link the gun to someone we know."

"How likely is that?"

"You ever see that TV show *Cold Case?* Well, we're working on a future episode."

CHAPTER NINETEEN

KAYLA LEAVES BASKETBALL practice and walks to the Honda Accord Remi bought for her. He'd made good on his promise to have it back to her right away.

She pulls onto the highway and drives the mile and a half to the Holy Redeemer Catholic Church. Entering through the main door, she walks straight down the aisle to the apse, where a white-haired priest is fiddling with something on the altar, she's not sure what.

"Are you Father Kane?"

He smiles. "Yes. Can I help you?"

"Where's your office?"

He glances to the robing room off the apse.

"Come on."

She walks onto the apse toward the robing room, nodding her head for the priest to follow her. He does and she leads him to the desk, taking one of the visitor chairs.

Once he's seated behind the desk, she looks around the room. "I thought the Catholic Church was supposed to have a lot of money."

"Not this one."

"I want to know what's going on with my dad."

He cocks his head.

"Remi Bone. And don't tell me you don't know who I'm talking about, because he told me he came to see you."

She stares into his eyes as she says this, finding darkness, telling her that whatever it is that's going on with Remi is bad.

"Is he fixing to become a drunk? He came home the other day with booze on his breath, and he told me he got it from you."

Lenny Kane looks down.

"That's a breach of the agreement."

"Agreement?"

"The deal he made with my mom. No booze. Beer's okay, but no liquor. He kept to that promise, until he met up with you."

"I apologize for that. I didn't know about the no-booze rule."

"And who exactly are you to Remi, anyway? He never mentioned you before."

"We go way back, to high school."

"You were friends? Couple a lunkheads messing around, talking trash, stealing the Boone's Farm, trying to get laid. Is that it?"

"Not exactly. We were both good fighters—"

"And what, you used to beat each other up? Or other kids? I guess I was right about the lunkhead part."

"Can you slow down a little? I can't listen as fast as you seem to be able to talk."

"Look. Here's the thing. I promised my mother I'd take care of him. I told her that on her deathbed. And I think I've been doing a pretty good job, up to you coming along. Which brings me back to my question. What's going on with Remi? Why did he come to see you?"

"It makes me happy to see that you love him as much as he does you. But I'm afraid I'm not at liberty to breach his confidence."

"What, he came to confession? He can't do that; he's not Catholic."

"It wasn't—"

"And since it's not a confession, it's not privileged."

"Your grasp of ecclesiastic law is quite . . . interesting. But I assure you, I cannot divulge the details of our discussion."

She glares at him.

"What I can say is that your father is very proud of you."

"I knew it! He's stressed out because of how much it's going to cost to send me to Penn. I told him I didn't have to go there. I was accepted at some other places and that would be fine with me. I told him that, and I meant it."

The look on the priest's face chills her.

"I did so mean it!"

"I think you should tell him again."

"I don't want him stressing out over money. He's not in the best of shape, you know. He doesn't exercise at all. He could have a heart attack, which happens all the time to men his age who are too sedentary."

An odd expression forms on the priest's face. Something about it upsets her. "What's that look?"

"I . . . didn't know I was making a *look*."

"Now you're just getting smart." She sits back, studies him for a moment. "You don't look like a priest. You look more like a Special Forces colonel, a hell-raiser, than a priest."

He smiles. "There was a time in my life when I'd have been glad to hear something like that," he says, his mind wandering back to when he was twenty-nine-years old, fresh from the first Gulf War and he and two of his friends decided to run the world looking for adventure. The three of them going to the islands and finding

beaches and fistfights and women, going to Europe and finding
Old World cities and fistfights and women, going to Africa, Soma-
lia, and finding . . . emaciated babies covered with flies. And one
day him holding one of those famine babies as it died in his arms,
and not letting go until he was made to, the whole thing striking
him like lightning, showing him what he needed to do with his
life. But his fear getting the better of him, and him racing for the
airport, trying to escape, but being stricken with malaria, dropping right there in the ticket line. Days of fever, passing in and out
of consciousness, until, finally, he said uncle, uttered the words he
knew God was waiting to hear: "Oh, all right."

Kayla interrupts the memories. "Are you going to tell me what's
up with Remi or not?"

The old priest opens his hands.

She stands and walks across the room, pausing in the doorway.
"I'll be back."

"Like the terminator," he says, but she doesn't hear because she's
gone.

CHAPTER TWENTY

LAUREN AND THE MAYOR sitting in the back of the Chevy Suburban sandwiched between two squad cars, the caravan moving along North Fifth Street toward the Rivera Recreation Center. They're on their way to meet with residents of the city's Fairhill and Kensington sections, upset that nothing's being done to clean up the notorious El Campamento.

"Every time I come up here, all I get is complaints. And I never have any good news to bring."

Lauren, looking out the window, doesn't answer.

Wallace Brown shifts in his seat. "Is there anything positive we can say to these people about their neighborhood?"

She turns to him. "We could cheer them up by reminding them that unemployment in Fairhill is 25 percent, and that's counting only the 40 percent who are in the labor market at all. Half the residents live below the poverty line, unless they're women, in which case, it's 60 percent, or children, in which case it's 72 percent. Twenty percent of the housing units are vacant; they call them 'abandominiums.' Or 'shooting galleries' because that's where a lot of addicts go to inject themselves."

"Why couldn't we have this meeting at City Hall?"

"Optics. It looks better if we go to them."

"Optics. God, I hate that word."

*   *   *

The cars pull into the lot and the mayor's entourage makes its way to the small gym, where folding chairs and a facing table have been set up. They're greeted with groans and boos as soon as they walk through the door, Wallace Brown smiling like he's being cheered.

They take their seats, and Lauren watches the mayor tell the group, "I want to thank you for agreeing to meet with me—"

"You didn't call us, we called you!" An angry male voice from one of the middle rows.

"—to discuss this terrible problem."

"When are you going to clean up El Campamento?" Another angry voice.

A young woman stands: "Mr. Mayor, my little girl goes to school every morning and looks down and sees people high on heroin just lying on the ground by the train tracks, like they're dead."

Wallace Brown shakes his head. "You're right. It's a terrible problem, and—"

"I have two young boys." A man is on his feet now. "I tell 'em not to go in there, but I know they do. I'm afraid they're going to get poked by a needle and get AIDS. It's only a matter of time before it happens, to them or someone else's kids."

"I hear you, believe me. I've been after those people at Conrail they own that whole area, you know. I've talked to them until I'm blue in the face, even threatened, but they won't clean it up. Makes me madder than hell." Here he balls his fist and punches his palm, showing them how upset he is, that he's on their side. And that he's manly.

Lauren struggles not to roll her eyes.

Two men on opposite sides of the room stand at the same time, the one on the right asking, "Why doesn't the city pay to clean it up?" The one on the left saying, "You found five million to dress up Dilworth Plaza for the rich people downtown."

The mayor explains that most of the cost for the plaza cleanup came from federal stimulus money and the Ritz-Carlton.

The meeting drags on for an hour, everyone getting angrier and more frustrated, until someone, a large man with a full beard, makes the threat: "You don't do something about this soon, we're going to take matters into our own hands."

Lauren and her boss exchange glances.

"The only reason," the man continues, "that you don't clear all those addicts outta that area and clean it up is 'cause it's up here and not in the business district. You get a bunch a them heroin zombies on your new plaza, or Rittenhouse, or Old City, and I guarantee the problem would be fixed."

"That's for damn sure!" Another angry voice.

"You said it!"

A chorus of anger.

"That went well." Back in the Chevy Suburban, Wallace Brown rubs his temples.

"He's right, you know," Lauren says. "We'd never tolerate a zombie apocalypse on Rittenhouse Square."

The mayor smiles. "Why not? We put up with it in city council."

Even Lauren smiles at that one.

CHAPTER TWENTY-ONE

NICK LOUGHEAD LOOKS across his desk at Jabes Santana. The Dominican, solidly built with gleaming black eyes, frankly frightens him. Clients like Jabes are the reason he keeps the Glock G31 Gen4 .357 with a fifteen-round magazine in his desk drawer.

"Your man did good," Jabes says, no smile on his face to match the praise. "One bullet, straight through the heart. A real pro, obviously. Want to tell me who he is?"

"I don't know who he is. Even the guy I deal with doesn't know. This is a real *whisper down the lane* situation."

"Whisper down the lane, eh?"

Jabes stares at Nick, whose mind is focused on his desk drawer, wondering how fast he could open it, pull out the pistol, aim and fire. Probably not fast enough. Jabes reaches into his coat pocket and Nick stiffens, until he sees that what the drug dealer is pulling out is just an envelope.

Jabes slides the envelope across the desk. "You want to count it?"

"No need. I trust you."

"That's the case, you're not as smart as I thought."

Nick starts to smile, but pulls it back, not sure what Jabes is looking for.

"So, this guy. You think he's hungry for more business?"

Nick pauses. *Stay cool. Don't seem too eager.*

"I don't know. I can ask."

Jabes nods. "You do that."

"Whether he's interested, and how much it'd cost, would depend on who you're looking to have taken care of."

They sit in silence for a moment, until Jabes says, "Let's say I had a partner, was trying to get a bigger piece than I think he deserves, trying to call the shots when it ain't his place."

"I'd ask why you don't take care of it yourself."

"That would cause a problem in the family. He's kind of like . . . my cousin."

"Kind of like."

"It would be bad for me to move against him myself. My mother, my uncle—I'd never hear the end of it."

"That is a problem. A bigger problem than Rolli Castillo. Bigger and with more risks. Cost a lot more to fix than thirty K."

"What if I said forty-five?"

"What if my guy says a hundred?"

Jabes glares at Nick. "You get the message to your guy, I'll pay seventy-five."

"I mean, I can tell him, but whether he jumps . . ."

"You just whisper down that lane of yours, and get back to me."

Jabes stands, turns to leave, and Nick calls out to him. "So, I can expect to hear from you the next time one of your guys gets locked up?"

"You get this thing done, I'll put you on retainer."

Nick watches him leave. When he's gone, he opens the envelope, spreads the bills across his desk, like playing cards, starts counting. Thirty thousand. He'll keep five as the finder's fee, give the rest to his uncle Deke, tell him about the new job.

He feels like celebrating so he pulls out his burner phone and calls Lauren.

"Hey, it's me. You up for something after work?"

"I can't. There's going to be a gun violence protest outside City Hall, on Dilworth Plaza, at five o'clock. It's being organized by the family of Dustin Ross. You know, the Drexel engineering student gunned down in Kensington."

"I know about him. Killed last year and the police still have no leads. His family's been raising cane in the press for months. Do you really think he was in the Badlands because he got lost?"

"Are you kidding? He was up there to score. Probably got shot because he said the wrong thing to the wrong street dealer."

"Hasn't your boss already met with the parents?"

"Three times. But they're still getting in front of the cameras every chance they get. So the mayor thinks he should go out and stand *with* the family and the protesters, complain about the police always dropping the ball on homicides."

"That sounds kind of—"

"Stupid? A sure way to get the police to hate him? That's what I keep telling him."

"So, could you meet me at, like, seven?"

"Sometimes, I swear, he doesn't listen to a word I say."

"Seven thirty?"

"I'm not in the mood."

"Is this a biology thing? Like next week would be better?"

"You're a moron."

The line goes dead and Nick puts the phone back in the desk drawer, next to the Glock. "Moody bitch." *Yeah, it's biology.*

CHAPTER TWENTY-TWO

ON THE SECOND morning after the killing, Remi parks his truck in the compound at Deke's Garage. It's a bright spring day, but the colors Remi sees are muted, almost gray, like those of a chilly cloud-covered day in November. Walking into the garage, he inhales the smells he's come to love, tire rubber, oil and grease, gasoline, but they don't register. Rufus Johnson, his best friend at work, waves and says hello, but Remi, his eyes straight ahead, doesn't see or hear him.

The feeling of diminishment he'd had when he stood before the mirror on the night of the killing has deepened. In a way, he seems compressed, like a three-dimensional object pressed flat. His senses feel flattened, too; he still sees, hears, tastes, smells, and feels, but everything is less intense, duller.

Numbed.

What's really worrying him, though, isn't the diminishment of his senses, but the guilt. The guilt he doesn't feel. He should feel terrible about what he's done, but he doesn't. He doesn't feel anything. *What's that say about me?*

"Hey, Bone!"

Shit.

It's Deke, standing by his door, waving him in.

When the door's shut and they're both seated, Deke says, "You ignored me all day yesterday. Something wrong? It shouldn't be. You did a damn fine job the other night. The man is happy as a pig in shit."

So, now it's "the man," Deke's contact. He shrugs.

"That guy you took care of was bad news. Sold bad H to young kids."

"That's what's making you smile? The public service part of it?"

"That, and *this*," he answers, pulling an envelope from his drawer and sliding it across the desk.

Remi doesn't move.

"Well, don't you want it?"

Remi sighs, takes the envelope, and stuffs it into his back pocket as he stands.

"What's your hurry? Don't you want to talk about it? Tell me how it went down?"

"How it went down? I shot him. What more you need to know?"

Deke shakes his head, exasperated. "Just give me a minute before you go running out of here." He nods toward the chair.

Remi sits. "What?"

"Thing is, you want it, there's another job."

It hangs in the air.

"Yours for the taking. More money, too." Deke smiles. "Total payout is seventy-five K. My guy gets ten, I get fifteen, you get the rest. Fifty K. The problem guy is another dealer, only he's a lot bigger fish than the first guy. As a matter of fact . . ."

Deke drones on about the dealer and what a good thing Remi would be doing to take him out, but Remi stopped listening when Deke said fifty K—enough for a full year of Kayla's tuition.

CHAPTER TWENTY-THREE

"CAN YOU EFFING believe this?" Rizzo sits at his desk, directly across from Flynn, his brown suit crumpled, noticing a small coffee stain on his white shirt, though that's not what's pissing him off.

"What?" Flynn says, looking up from a report he's typing, neither one of them thinking about the Rolli Castillo case, only three days old and already destined for the bottom drawer of a dusty file cabinet.

Looking down now at the *Daily News*: "Mayor shit-head's opioid task force just came back with its recommendations to solve the heroin crisis. Guess what one of their ideas is?"

Flynn stares.

"Safe-injection sites. Places where heroin users can come for clean needles to stick themselves with."

"You're shitting me."

"New needles, plus access to naloxone, to save them from overdosing."

Flynn chuckles. "Maybe we should set up lemonade and cookie stands for them. Show them movies."

"What's next, safe robbery sites? Places where people can get robbed without being shot or stabbed."

"That's where I'd go to get robbed."

"Assholes." Rizzo crumples the paper, tosses it into the trash can. Just then, he sees the captain, Sharon Walker, enter the lieutenant's office and shut the door.

Five minutes later, the door opens and the lieutenant sticks his head out. "Rizzo! You, too, Flynn."

They stand and walk to the office, take seats in front of the desk while the lieutenant closes the door.

Rizzo looks at the captain, flaming red hair, tall and still fit in her early forties. "You're looking lovely today, Captain Walker." Rizzo smiles.

"Screw you, Ed."

He'd love to say it: *You did. Many times. Back when I was still drinking and you a lowly patrol officer.*

"We have a problem," the lieutenant says, taking his chair. "Ballistics came back on the Castillo case."

"It's Mr. Smith," says Sharon Walker.

Rizzo sits up. "Damn."

Flynn looks puzzled. "Who's Mr. Smith?"

"Not who," Rizzo says. "What. The gun used in the shooting. A Smith & Wesson Model 686, fixed sight, six-round revolver with a six-inch barrel. Fires .357 Magnum or .38 Specials. Been used in thirty-one unsolved homicides going back twenty years."

"Whoa."

"It's one of the biggest secrets in the department," says Captain Walker. "And it needs to stay that way."

Rizzo, leaning in to his partner: "You see, Pat, we're very sensitive to anything that would call attention to our 54 percent unsolved homicide rate. Such as the same gun being used for two decades to mow down dozens of our citizens."

"Can it, Ed."

Sharon Walker's voice is acid, reminding Rizzo of their frequent fights, and the volcanic makeup sex that always followed. He sees Sharon, naked, her tiny boobs and rock-solid body from all the working out she did, standing with her arms on her narrow hips, ripping into him. Sees her an hour later soaked with sweat, riding him hard, moaning, grunting.

"The point is," says the lieutenant, "the Castillo case is now priority one."

"Zero to hero," says Rizzo.

Flynn chuckles.

"You want to be pounding the pavements again, Flynn?" The lieutenant is on his feet now. "This is serious. I want whoever shot Castillo to be found. And I want that goddamned gun off the streets. Oh, and Ed? I see you spending an hour reading the *Daily News* again, you'll be doing undercover work at gay bars."

* * *

Back at their desks, Flynn asks Rizzo for more background on Mr. Smith.

"Bad boy's done it all. Half-a-dozen drive-bys; liquor store, bank and convenience store hold-ups; robbery-murders of a jewelry courier, a pizza delivery man, a surgeon out by HUP; an armored car heist; and last but not least, Dustin Ross, the college kid murdered up in Fairhill."

Flynn takes it all in. "How is it possible that the same gun's been used for all those crimes?"

"Not hard to understand. Guy uses the gun to hold up a liquor store, kills the clerk. Gun's hot now, so he sells it or gives it to someone else, who uses it to rob a bank. That guy's brother-in-law or cousin says he needs a gun to use on some doctor been banging his wife, does the guy know anyone who has one? He says, sure, but get rid of it once you're done because it's hot. The guy shoots the doctor, maybe hides the gun or maybe gives it to a friend and so on down the lane. The possible permutations are endless."

"But the odds of no one getting arrested in all this time . . ."

"About the same as winning the Powerball, which someone does every couple a weeks."

Flynn nods his head, thinks a while. Then, "There's still one thing I don't understand. That gay bar thing the lieutenant threatened you with. How can it be undercover if everyone there knows you?"

Rizzo smiles. "Wow. That was a good one. You really might have a future around here."

CHAPTER TWENTY-FOUR

"I HAVE A HEADACHE." The honorable Wallace Brown leans over his desk, rubbing his temples. "Why don't you fix me something?"

"Sure thing, boss." Lauren Devereux moves toward the minibar. The mayor's been in a foul mood for two days, since the protest against the city's unsolved murder rate outside City Hall led by the family of Dustin Ross. She'd prevailed on him not to make an ass of himself by joining the protesters. But she hadn't been able to talk him out of a fourth meeting with the parents, which turned into a disaster when they brought a Fox 29 news crew to his office. The lambasting went on for forty minutes and was captured in its entirety on video, the worst parts replayed on every news cycle since.

She walks to the desk, hands him the tumbler.

Wallace Brown gulps down a big swallow of scotch. "I don't know what I'd do without..."

Me?

"... this stuff. Sometimes, I swear God himself invented booze because he knew what a shit-fest life would turn out to be for everyone."

"An inspiring thought."

"I have to get out from under this. Almost three hundred murders, more than half unsolved—"

"That's not your fault. It's the police de—" She cuts herself off, too late.

"As I'd have pointed out if you'd let me join the protest the other night."

"A mayor joining protesters against the police would be terrible optics."

"Optics." Spitting out the word. "What time is it? Can I leave yet? And please don't tell me I have to make an appearance tonight at some charity event or . . ." He trails off, too tired to finish.

"No events this evening. And just one more appointment—she's waiting outside. Captain Sharon Walker. The commissioner sent her over, said you'll want to hear what she has to say."

"What was his excuse for not coming himself?"

"I'll get the captain," she says, making for the door.

A moment later, she ushers in the attractive police officer and watches as the mayor smiles broadly, gets up from his desk, trying to be sly about eyeing her up and down as he extends his hand.

"Captain . . . Walker, is it? Nice to meet you. Please, have a seat."

Everyone sits and Sharon Walker gets right to it. "The chief, at the commissioner's request, asked me to come and tell you that we may have a break in the Dustin Ross case."

"Oh?" The mayor sitting at attention now.

"The gun used to kill Ross was recently used to gun down a drug dealer up in the Badlands."

Lauren glances at her boss. "So, you think there's a connection between the two deaths?"

"We're looking into it."

"Would you like something to drink?" Wallace Brown starts to rise from his seat, to fetch some scotch, something he's not done for Lauren since she'd rebuffed his advances shortly after she was hired.

"I'm on the job." The captain holds up her hand.

"Right. Of course." The disappointment plain on his face.

"Any other information on the gun?" Lauren asks.

"Only that it was used in both killings."

"Should we make an announcement?" asks the mayor.

"No." Lauren and the captain both fire at once.

"Best not to tip our hands, just yet," says Sharon Walker. "It would upset the Ross family if we revealed the link between the two killings, and it turned into a dead end."

"Pardon the pun." The mayor smiles at his wit.

Lauren smiles, too. "Good one, sir." *I hate myself.*

"So, is this really a development, then?"

"Well, Mr. Mayor, like I said, it could be. And there's enough of a chance that the commissioner wanted to make sure you were told about it right away." *To get you off his back.*

"Uh-huh." Wallace Brown glances sideways at Lauren, who sees that he finally gets that the commissioner is just blowing smoke.

They talk some more, the mayor offering to appoint the red-headed captain as police department liaison to a committee Lauren's never heard of. Lauren squints, signaling to the attractive policewoman that the offer is bullshit.

Sharon says she'll get back to Wallace Brown and the meeting ends quickly, the mayor's eyes fixed on her tight behind as she walks to the door.

Lauren closes the door and turns to her boss.

"Really?"

"What?"

CHAPTER TWENTY-FIVE

REMI AND KAYLA at the breakfast table, him with a big plate of scrambled eggs and melted cheese, her crunching from a bowl of Special K.

"That cereal's nothing but air," he says.

"Those eggs and cheese are nothing but a heart attack."

Remi stops his fork in midair, not having thought about that before. He'd have to call Chuckie Paxton again, ask him if a better diet would hold off the heart failure, but figuring it wouldn't because it wasn't like he had clogged arteries.

"You could at least mix in some spinach or broccoli."

He puts the fork down and lifts a glass of orange juice to his mouth, feeling her looking at him, something she does all the time now, watching him like a hawk, ever since the day he'd come home with booze on his breath. He'd even caught her this morning going through his drawers.

"What were you looking for, in my room?" he says.

"You know what."

"I told you the booze was a onetime thing."

"And then you came home way after midnight with puke on your breath and some cock and bull story about working late."

"We going to have a problem you keep talking to me like this."

"I'm just looking out for you, Remi. For both of us."

This stops him again. "*You* looking out for *me*?"

"There's spinach and tomatoes in the fridge," she says, taking his plate. "I'm going to make you some healthy eggs."

He watches her scrape his plate and unload the fridge, but his mind is back in the Badlands, seeing the lifeless eyes of Rolli Castillo, his facial muscles slack, his limp limbs making him look like a rag doll. He searches himself, this new, lesser him, for a reaction and finds none, the killing feeling neither good nor bad, but as just something that happened.

"Here, eat these."

"Where's the cheese?"

"No cheese. I mixed in skim milk instead. See how fluffy it looks?"

He sits back, smiles, remembering. "That's just how your mother made them for me."

She reaches out, touches his hand. *See. I'm taking care of you, just like I promised Mom.*

*   *   *

An hour later, Remi's in Deke's office, staring at his boss.

"So, there's two guys I'm supposed to handle this time?"

"No. Well, sure, there's going to be two guys, but you're only supposed to whack the one. This one here," he says, sliding forward a black-and-white photograph. "His name's Saulo. Saulo Rodriguez."

"Saulo." He repeats the name, liking the way it rolls off his tongue.

"Now, Saulo, he's going to be with his cousin Jabes, which is this guy." Deke slides a second photo across his desk.

"Wait. You want me to shoot this guy in front of his cousin?"

"Well, you got to shoot both of them. But Jabes, you only shoot a little—"

"Shoot *a little*? The fuck are you talking about?"

"See, Jabes is the one hiring you. He's got to get his cousin out of the family business. But he can't let his relatives know he's involved, so it has to look like someone tried to kill him, too. So you shoot Jabes, but only, say, graze him—"

"This is getting crazier by the minute."

"No, it makes perfect sense, you think about it."

"Thinking about this makes me want to shoot you."

Deke stares.

"Seriously. If I shoot what's his name, Saulo, in front of this Jabes, what's to stop Jabes from fingering me to the police, he gets in trouble down the line?"

"Because he'd have to admit it was him who set the whole thing up. And he knows if they brought you in, you could say so."

"I don't like it. You got to figure out some other way. You and Jabes."

Deke exhales. "Remi, what can I tell you. It's how he wants it to go down. And you'll be getting fifty grand." He reaches into his desk drawer, pulls out a thick envelope. "The first ten of which is right here."

Remi stares at the yellow envelope, which, for some reason reminds him of the eggs Kayla cooked him that morning. Kayla, who's going to go to an Ivy League college and won't ever have to cook for anyone but her husband and kids.

He reaches across the desk, takes the envelope. "And where is this all supposed to take place?"

"Ever hear of El Campamento?"

CHAPTER TWENTY-SIX

"I CAN'T BELIEVE I let this happen."

Rizzo, on the bed, hands behind his head on the pillow, watching her dress in the middle of the room, says, "Let it happen? You called me."

"To talk about the case. Dustin Ross, and Castillo, and the gun. My meeting with the mayor."

"A meeting which was pure bullshit. And which took you all of two minutes to explain to me."

"Where're my panties?"

"I threw them somewhere. You could've told me about the meeting over the phone."

"You're complaining?"

"No way," he says, remembering her call, telling him to meet her at "the old place," the Berwyn Tavern, where they used to hook up. It was far enough from the city they'd never be seen together and conveniently located a few minutes up Lancaster Avenue from the Marriott Courtyard in Devon.

"I figured you were dyeing your hair, but I see that's not the case," he says, looking at the little patch of red at the top of her legs.

She glances down. "I'm told a lot of the younger girls are shaving themselves completely bald. That's not for me."

"Me neither. I don't want to feel like I'm with some twelve-year-old."

"I bet you wish I was a little bit younger, though, eh? Twenty-six again, instead of forty-one."

"Nah. I like the older ones. A few dents and dings don't bother me."

She glares at him. "Dents and dings, huh? You take a look at yourself lately?"

"I'm not that bad."

"Ha!"

He pauses. "How's Marv?"

Her face sours. "He actually told a joke last night. I think it was his first one."

"No shit. Was it good? What was it about?"

"I don't know. It had to do with numbers. I guess it was an actuarial joke."

"You sure it was a joke?"

"I assumed so. He was smiling when he finished." She stops dressing for a moment, then finishes putting on her captain's uniform.

"I never figured out what you saw in him."

"Stability."

"Such a fun word."

"More fun than waking up naked and hungover in the back of my squad car with a nitwit detective, almost ruining my career before it even got started."

He searches for something clever to say when his cell rings. He sits up, puts his feet on the floor, looks at the number. "Now what? Jesus."

"Who was that?" she asks when he hangs up.

"Assisted living."

"Your mother? She still calling herself Elise?"

"It's Leeza now."

"She was always a piece of work, as I recall."

"She's fighting with half the women in the home. The director just told me she pretended to make up with one of them, got them both an Uber to Pottstown—"

"What's in Pottstown?"

"Nothing. Soon as they got there and the other lady got out of the car, Leeza told the driver to take her back to the home. Told him the other woman's son was going to pick her up on the corner."

"Leeza. I like it."

"It's not her name."

"So what happened to the other woman?"

"She stood on the street for an hour, until a cop drove by, asked her if she was okay."

"And now the old folks home is threatening to kick your mother out. That it?"

"I like that you call it an old folks home."

"You know I'm a plain talker."

"I like that, too." He smiles. "So, are we on again?"

"Forget it. This was a onetime thing."

"How come? I thought what we just had was pretty good."

"It was good. That part of us was always good. I'll think about it. But if I see you again, you're going to have to start taking better care of yourself. I mean, look at you. What are you, thirty pounds overweight? Forty? It's disgusting."

"You weren't complaining a half hour ago."

"I wasn't thinking straight."

"Part of being a redhead, isn't it?"

She throws one of his shoes at him and leaves.

CHAPTER TWENTY-SEVEN

MIDNIGHT. REMI WAITS again behind the gate at Buford's Garage. The blue Subaru pulls up and he leaves the compound, gets inside.

"Good to see you, sir." Virgil's smile is genuine.

Remi takes the kid in again, taking note of the white teeth and blond hair. This time, the kid is wearing a powder blue button-down shirt over chinos.

"I'd hoped you'd be out of this business by now."

"Sadly, no. But maybe someday."

"I'd love to know what you did that made you owe somebody this big."

"You don't want to hear it, sir. It's a long story, and all very sordid, I'm afraid."

Remi shakes his head. "Let's go. Get this done."

Virgil pulls away and Remi opens the glove compartment, takes out the gun, checks it out, same as he did the first time. He frowns and pulls out his cellphone, dials Deke.

"What the hell, Deke. You having me use the same gun?"

"What? No. It's not the same. Shouldn't be, anyhow. My guy said he instructed the other one be tossed into the river."

"I'm telling you it's the same gun."

Silence at the other end.

"So, I get caught and I'm connected to two shootings."

"I hear you, man. But I was told—"

He hangs up, looks at Virgil. "Anyone tell you to get rid of this gun after I used it the first time?"

"No."

"Unbelievable."

"If we had more time, I could take you to a friend of mine has lots of guns, and other stuff, too. He's across the bridge, in Camden."

Other stuff too? "Just take me to that campamento place." Remi shivers, remembering the trash and broken furniture, needles all over the ground, the scattered bodies. Bodies of half-living men and women, so tripped out it didn't bother them to lie outside all night long. Half an hour later, Remi looks around as Virgil stops the car on the East Gurney side of the B Street Bridge.

"Now, listen. I got on the Google last night and pulled this place up. The best thing for you to do while I'm meeting these guys under the bridge is to go down to A Street, then come up Tusculum. Drive real slow. You should be getting back here just as I'm done. I'll climb up the embankment on the Tusculum side. You meet me at the top. Got it?"

"That sounds perfect, sir."

"No Ubering this time, you hear me?"

"I'll be right there, waiting."

Remi stares at the kid, then leaves the car, carrying a leather case that's supposed to be full of heroin, the invented reason for the meeting. Jabes told his cousin Saulo that he found a new source of the drug, not Mexican, but a guy from down South.

It's darker tonight than it was the first time he was there, and he has to be especially careful walking down the embankment. At the bottom, by the tracks, he looks to his right, sees a match ignite under the bridge, someone lighting a cigarette. His signal.

He walks beneath the bridge, finds two men, one taller than the other, both solid. Problem is their faces look the same to him, in the bad light. He stands before them, holding the bag, looking from one to the other.

"Which one of you's Jabes?"

"I am," says the shorter one.

"Or maybe it's me," says the other one, smiling, trying to be funny or maybe already smelling a rat—Remi's not sure which.

"Fuck it," says the shorter one, obviously not in the mood for games. "He's Saulo; he's the one you're here to waste."

"Whoa!" Saulo now on full alert, his hands up, takes a half-step back. "What the fuck, Cousin."

"I told you, back off the business, *Cousin.* But you don't listen."

Remi, the revolver now pointing at Saulo, gets ready to say the words, pull the trigger.

"You going to shoot me in front of him?" Saulo says. "That the plan? Pretty stupid, having a witness."

Jabes shakes his head. "He knows I can't ever talk without it coming back to me." Then, to Remi, "Come on, man, pull the trigger."

"My old man's going to kill you for this," Saulo says.

"Nah, this one's gonna shoot me, too. Just graze me, so it looks like we was both set up."

"That what he tell you?" Saulo looking at Remi. "That he's going to let you shoot him? You're a fool, man. He's going to wait 'til you off me, then shoot you himself, be the hero to the family. Look, he's reaching back now."

One glance at Jabes tells Remi that Saulo is right.

"Tick tock says the clock."

He fires.

"Time's up, motherfuck."

He fires again.

Two shots straight through the heart and Jabes and Saulo are both on the ground, spurting blood like oil geysers into the cool moist air.

"I knew this wasn't going to work." He shakes his head, walks out from under the bridge and makes his way up the hill to the waiting Subaru Legacy.

"Perfect timing, sir!"

"Just get me the hell outta here."

"Something go wrong down there?"

"Nothing I shouldn't 'a seen coming."

The ride back is a long one, and quiet. When they reach the garage, Remi considers for a moment what to do with the gun. He decides to put it back into the glove compartment, after he wipes off his prints.

"I don't want to see this gun again, you hear me?"

"I don't blame you."

"You tell your boss to get rid of it. He gives you any problem, you throw it in the river yourself."

"Well..."

"I mean it. This gun's carrying the names of three dead men. It's bad luck to keep it. Bad luck and stupid."

He shoots a hard look at Virgil, then leaves the car. Just as Virgil begins to pull away, Remi turns and shouts, "Wait." Leaning through the passenger door window, he opens the glove compartment, pulls out the gun. "I'm getting rid of this damn thing myself. That way I'll know for sure it's gone."

He enters the compound, walks to his F-150, and locks the gun in the aluminum truck bed toolbox.

*   *   *

Fifteen minutes later, he walks through his front door, flops down on his easy chair. Kayla won't be confronting him this time, her being away for the night at a student leadership thing in Washington. Still, he sees her face like she's standing right there. Hears her saying, "You want to tell me what's going on?"

"You'll never find out," he says aloud.

It'd break her heart, and he can't have that. He looks up at the fireplace mantel, stands and walks over to it, to the pictures. Bea and him at their wedding. Bea and him and Kayla at the beach. Bea all dressed up to go to a reunion of her college nursing class. This last one he picks up and stares at for a long time, his eyes watering.

The love of his life. The navigator who guided him along the straight and narrow. Gone now, and look at what he's doing. Good for so long, and now worse than he ever was. And worse yet, not seeming to have a problem with it, his conscience feeling like it'd been stripped from him.

"Oh, Bone." He shakes his head. "What're you making of yourself?"

CHAPTER TWENTY-EIGHT

SEVEN A.M. Rizzo and Flynn standing under the B Street Bridge. Flynn says, "Can you believe this place? It looks like a war zone."

"War zones are nicer."

"All this shit, the trash, the furniture, and these needles. Why doesn't the city clean this place up?"

"These two," Rizzo says. "Bullets straight through the heart, just like Castillo."

"You think it's the same guy? Same gun?"

"We'll know soon enough. I'll tell the lieutenant to put some pressure on, get ballistics back sooner rather than later." Thinking: I'll also give Sharon a call, use it as a reason to get together again.

"You think he was lying in wait for them, like with Castillo?"

Rizzo studies the bodies. "Nah. I think they were all standing here together, the three of them, talking. He pulls out his gun. Pop. Pop."

"Tick tock says the clock."

Rizzo and Flynn look at each other. Rizzo says, "The fuck was that?"

"I think it came from that pile of clothes." Flynn points to a mound about fifteen feet away, near the wall supporting the bridge.

"That's not just clothes," Rizzo says, walking over.

"The hell?" says Flynn.

"Heroin zombie."

Flynn looks down at the glazed eyes.

Rizzo nudges the zombie with his foot. "Hey, buddy, what'd you say?"

Nothing.

"Tick tock, was it?"

The zombie's eyes clear a little. "Tick tock says the clock. Time's up, motherfuck."

"You think he was here when those two got it?" asks Flynn. "Tick tock, time's up is what he was thinking when it went down?"

"Maybe not what he was thinking. Maybe what he was hearing."

"That'd be kind of weird, if the killer said that."

"You ever see *Pulp Fiction*?"

"No, but I heard it was good. Why?"

"Good? It's great. You should rent it. Look for Samuel L. Jackson."

Rizzo refocuses on the zombie. "Hey. You see who shot those guys?"

"Tick tock says the clock—"

"Yeah, yeah. We got it." Rizzo shakes his head.

"Should we take him in?" asks Flynn.

"You want this thing in our car? I can barely stand the reek out here in the open."

"Still, we should call dispatch."

"And say what? There's a guy up here at El Campamento, looks like he's been taking drugs?"

Rizzo turns and walks toward the paramedics standing nearby, waiting for him and Flynn to finish. "All yours, guys. Bag and tag."

*   *   *

Already lunchtime and Deke still a no-show at the garage. Remi's steaming, having waited all morning to ream him out for the knucklehead plan that took him to the B Street Bridge and made him end up knocking off two guys instead of just one. He still can't believe he agreed to whack a guy in front of a witness.

He turns to see Deke walking fast toward his office, moves to intercept the old man.

"I know! I know." Deke holding up his hands, shaking his head, as he zips across the floor.

Remi follows him into the office, closes the door, and waits for Deke to sit down, before leaning over the desk at him. "You got any notion how pissed I am?"

"Me too, man. Me too."

"I don't suppose I'm going to get paid, now that the guy who hired us is dead."

"Jabes didn't hire us. My guy hired us. Jabes hired him."

Remi thinks on this. "If *your guy* is the one who hired us, then he can pay up."

Deke's eyes widen. "How? Jabes was supposed to pay him."

"You're telling me I wacked two guys for a measly 10K—"

"Better'n I did. My share was all coming out of the back end—"

"I'm out forty thousand."

"I hear you, brother."

"*Brother?*"

"You know what I mean. Look, I get it, you're upset, and you have every right to be. But I'll make it up to you, on the next job. I promise."

"I didn't want there to be a next job. The money I'd have made on this one, I was going to quit."

Deke stares.

"So, the next job's got to make up for it. What I lost this time, plus money to cover the next. You got that?"

"Yeah, sure."

"And I want it all up front."

"Up front? How can—"

"And get me a different goddamned gun!"

Remi points his finger across the desk, then straightens up, turns, and leaves. Behind him, Deke is saying something, but he ignores him.

CHAPTER TWENTY-NINE

FATHER LENNY KANE is still upset by what he'd learned that morning on Fox News—two men shot to death up in the Badlands. Drug dealers killed in the middle of the night, the paper saying it might be linked to a similar murder committed the week before.

Is Remi Bone the one doing it? He can't be sure. But he is. A failure on his part, not getting through to the man.

He sighs, thinking back on their conversation, to the part where Bone asked if it mattered that the man he was going to kill was a drug dealer, and him hesitating before saying, "No."

He shouldn't have paused. It was automatic, though, his mind traveling back to a day twelve years before, when he stood over the body of a government official in Niger. He was thirty-nine, three years a priest. He'd been in Africa for two years, living through the drought and the locusts that'd devoured almost all of the crops. For years, the official, a local tyrant, had stolen aid relief meant to help feed the starving. Some people in the village tried to fight back, and the official had several of them beaten, one almost to death. It was too much for him to take, so he confronted the official late one night, the official laughing at him in his priest outfit. The official pushing him. The official pushing him harder. The official falling dead onto the ground after receiving a punch to the gut that lifted him three feet in the air.

A terrible lapse on his part. A failure that made him question his right to be a priest, made him leave Africa, where his heart was, where he felt he could really help, and come home to shepherd a flock whose trials and tribulations were mostly self-inflicted.

Lenny Kane finds himself pulling his car into Remi Bone's driveway just before six p.m. He sees Remi watching him from the front porch, where he's sitting on a wooden rocking chair, drinking a beer.

He takes his time walking through the yard and up the steps. He nods toward Remi's Budweiser, says, "Don't mind if I do," and waits for Bone to fetch him a can.

They sit and drink for a while, neither saying anything, until he asks, "How's the heart?"

Remi blinks, not sure how to take it. "Still working okay, I guess. You know, tick tock."

"I was watching the news this morning. About those two guys shot in the Fairhill section."

"The drug dealers?"

"Seems the police think the killings might be related to that shooting a week ago."

"Seems you think that, too."

He waits for Remi to admit or deny it. When he doesn't, he says, "Funny thing. The other day, I got a visit from a young woman who thinks her father is in some kind of trouble. Found out he came to see me, so she figured maybe I knew what was going on."

Remi's eyes widen. "Kayla?"

"The name she gave me."

"What'd you tell her?"

"Nothing I could tell her. Confessional privilege."

Remi squints.

"She didn't buy it, either."

"She's worried I'm drinking liquor—something I promised her mother I wouldn't do. Something I didn't do, till I came to see you."

"Have you given any thought to what I told you, about remorse?"

Remi nods his head yes.

"And?"

He watches Remi rub his chest.

"Maybe your ticker's not working the way it should be. Is that what you're telling me?"

Remi takes a sip of the Bud. "You think lack of guilt can be a symptom of heart disease?"

"More likely it's a symptom of soul disease."

Remi takes a deep breath. "I may be in worse trouble than I thought."

Lenny Kane finishes his beer, says, "You fix cars, right? Mind taking a look at mine?"

Remi glances at the red Buick LeSabre, figuring it for a 2010. "You having a problem with it?"

"It's kind of sluggish. Moves like a guy who just woke up with a bad hangover."

He sees Remi smile, both of them knowing just what he means by waking up with a hangover. He follows Remi to the driveway, where Bone opens the hood. Still in his work jeans and t-shirt, the mechanic pulls a rag from his back pocket, uses it to clean the dipstick.

"When's the last time you changed the oil in this thing?"

"I bought it used two years ago. Haven't taken it in yet," he answers.

"Bring it by the shop tomorrow. I'll change the oil, put in some new plugs. A new fan belt."

"How much will all that set me back?"

"It'll be on the house."

"I hope you do a better job setting this car right than I've done with you." He looks the other man in the eye as he says this, seeing Remi's own eyes looking past him.

He hears another car approaching, turns and sees the Honda Accord parking in front of the house. Kayla opens the door, walks toward them.

"Well, well. If it isn't Father Kane. Your old friend I never heard of before."

"Your daughter paid me a visit the other day."

"That right?"

"Seems to think you're in some kind of trouble."

Kayla's face darkens. "I know something's going on. And I know he told you what it is," she says to the priest. Then, to Remi: "He wouldn't tell me. Claims it's privileged. Which is a load of you-know-what."

Remi frowns. "I told you there's nothing to worry about."

"Says the man who all of a sudden shows up at church for the first time in years. And then comes home reeking of booze."

Father Kane watches the girl, standing arms akimbo, standing up to her father, impressed by her self-assurance, the tone of her voice. His own eyes still on her, he tells Remi, "This is one confident young woman you're raising here."

"Don't patronize me," she says, turning to walk into the house. Then turning back, telling them both she's got her eyes on them.

Once she's inside, Remi tells him, "She's special. Now you can see why I'm willing to go out on a limb for her."

"I get it, Bone. But that's not a limb you're sitting on. It's a skewer. And if you don't get off it, you'll end up a toasted marshmallow."

Remi considers this. "I don't suppose I could get out of it by saying a thousand Hail Marys."

"Without remorse, prayers won't work any better than jumping jacks."

Remi takes a deep breath, tries to drum up some guilt. But there's nothing there.

CHAPTER THIRTY

"I'M SORRY," NICK SAYS. "I'm just distracted. It's not your fault."

"No shit it's not." Lauren Devereux is angry.

"It's just, some bad stuff went down at work today." Bad as in he turned on the news that morning to learn the hit man he hired had killed his client. Now there'd be no more money. And his master plan to use Jabes and the Dominicans as a stepping stone to connect with the Mexican cartels smashed to pieces. And some unpaid executioner out there undoubtedly pissed as hell at him and looking for his money.

"I can't believe I wore garters and you react like I'm some spread-assed fishwife in a housecoat and curlers."

He sits up in bed, but she continues before he can talk.

"It's the heels, isn't it? They're too much."

"No. I love stilettos." And he does, the way they make her calf muscles bulge, make her long legs even longer. "You're smoking hot. You know that."

"So why am I standing here in the middle of the room, half-naked, while you sit on the bed with Little Nicky hanging like a dead tadpole?"

"That never happened before!"

"Now you're making me feel really special." She turns toward the bathroom, gathering her clothes on the way.

He sits with his knees drawn up, his mind fixed on the angry killer with the one-shot-straight-through-the-heart accuracy. He rocks back and forth.

She walks out of the bathroom, shakes her head. "God, I hate myself."

He hears her leave, slam the door behind her. Then he reaches to the bed-stand for his cellphone.

*   *   *

Deacon Buford picks up the phone. "Yeah?"

"It's me," says the voice at the other end, his nephew, Nick.

"What a screwup," Deke says, getting out ahead of it, what he knows is coming, what he prepared for.

"What the hell was he thinking, your man?"

"What was he thinking? Well, gee, Nick, I guess he was thinking he better shoot Jabes before Jabes shoots him."

"That wasn't going to happen."

"My guy says he could see it in the Dominican's eyes. Says he saw your Jabes guy ready to go for his own gun."

"Well, now what?" asks Nick.

"You mean what's my guy looking for? He's looking to get paid, and since he ended up shooting two guys, he wants twice the amount he agreed to for the one."

"How am I supposed to come up with that kind of money?"

"Only one way I can think of," Deke says, making the play he'd mapped out. "You got to find another job, a big one, pays enough to make up for him getting stiffed on those two he took care of under the bridge."

"But I just lucked into that hit for Jabes, same as the job up by the No-Name. I'm not the kind of guy goes out looking to set up this kind of thing."

"This is not a guy to cross."

"But it's not my fault. I—"

"It'd kill your mother, my sister, something happened to you."

"I can't believe this."

Deke smiles, liking the panic in his nephew's voice. The snarky lawyer making fun of him at family picnics, saying NASCAR is a hick show, insinuating with his tone that the kid didn't believe he'd ever raced cars to begin with.

"Look, you want me to tell him to go screw himself, that you ain't paying?"

"I didn't say that."

Deke waits.

"Look, tell him I'll get back to you."

"I'll hold him off long as I can," Deke says.

Deke hangs up the phone and chuckles, the idea that Remi would go after Nick being ridiculous.

Sitting back in his chair, he looks through the windows that make up the top half of his inside office wall, windows installed so he can watch his mechanics, make sure they're not jerking off. The bays are empty now, it being close to eight p.m. He knows his wife will be waiting for him to get home, doing her best to keep his dinner warm, probably something special, for their anniversary. He leans over, opens his bottom desk drawer, pulls out a bottle of Jack Daniel's. There's a glass in the drawer and he pulls that out, too, sits it on the desk. He unscrews the lid on the whiskey, his movements slow, deliberate, him being in no hurry.

*   *   *

Nick paces the room, still in his t-shirt and boxers. "Not good," he says aloud. Not good having an assassin furious with him and looking for money. What a stupid damned thing it was to serve himself up to Jabes as a Murder, Inc. middleman. Dumber still to arrange a hit where the client wants to be there himself.

"Shit, shit, shit."

And now he has no choice but to go out and beat the bushes for a job that pays so well Uncle Deke's guy will overlook being cheated out of fifty thousand—no, wait, a hundred thousand—dollars.

He has to figure some way out of the mess he's in, but instead of ideas and plans and strategies, his mind keeps landing on women. He sees Katie, his first girlfriend, sweet and shy, making him turn off all the lights before she'd let him take off her clothes. Debbie, her younger sister, who'd suck him off in the basement rec room while he waited for Katie to get ready for their dates. The long line of girls he had sex with in college, seeing their faces but not remembering their names. His wife, Amy, and the dozen or so other women he'd slept with after they were married, women like Lauren, his perennial friend-with-benefits, and that other brunette, his ex-secretary, what's-her-name. And...

"Maleena! That's it!"

He pivots, grabs his cell, and dials.

"Oh, please be there. Please be there. Please be there."

"I love to hear a man beg," the voice at the other end cuts in. A voice strong and smoky, and with that Russian accent he'd always found irresistible.

He takes a deep breath to steady himself, then says the word he'd whisper in her ear when they made love, the word that always set her off: "Maleena." Her name.

He hears her take a deep drag from her cigarette, knows she's trying to figure out the best approach to take with him, the best angle.

"I knew you'd come crawling back," she says.

"I wasn't the one who walked away," he says, remembering one night in bed when she said she couldn't see him anymore, said she didn't feel right cheating on her husband. He'd said sure, no problem, he understood, showing how cool he was, knowing by then that she'd been seen spending time with one of the Phillies.

"Ah, what was I thinking?"

"That you found a man with a better bat."

Silence on the other end; she doesn't get it.

"How are things with you and Doctor Hal?" he asks, referring to her husband, Harold Roseman, the celebrated physician-entrepreneur running three of the city's biggest substance abuse clinics, supposedly helping people beat addiction, but in reality places where everyone goes to pick up prescriptions for Suboxone and Klonopin, which they then sell on the streets. The practice brings in millions and Hal and Maleena, his twenty-five-year-old wife and former Pilates instructor, live like royalty. But that's all going to end soon, word on the street being that Hal is already under indictment and getting ready to plead.

"Don't pretend you don't know."

"I feel bad."

"For my husband?"

"For you."

She sighs. "I feel bad for me, too."

"How about we get together," he says. "I may have a way to save you from losing everything."

Another drag of the cigarette, Winston if he remembers right. She's thinking, he can tell.

"Why not?" she says.

They agree to meet for a drink in the downstairs bar at the Ritz, their old stomping grounds. If things go well, he knows they'll head upstairs. And he'll have a way to fix his problem with the hit man.

He hangs up the phone, sits on the bed, and closes his eyes, letting his mind play Google satellite on Maleena's body. He starts with the distance shot of her, tall and rock solid, broad shoulders over thin hips, then zooms in for a flyby of her generous breasts, making sure to get a good look at her large pink areolas before heading south to the tuft of white-blond hair between her long, sculpted legs.

He reaches for himself . . . just in time to be ripped from his reverie by loud knocking on the door.

Is it him? The killer?

No, it couldn't be. Deke says the guy is still figuring on getting paid. And how would the killer know where he was, the apartment belonging to his capo client. Still, his heart is pounding as he walks toward the door, wishing it had an eyehole.

He holds his breath and slowly opens the door to find Lauren standing on the other side, an angry look on her face.

"This is bullshit," she says, pushing her way past him. "Nobody goes soft on me." She stops and turns, nods toward the bed. "Let's go—get your shorts off. I'm horny."

CHAPTER THIRTY-ONE

RIZZO ROLLS OFF of her, huffing and puffing. "We keep this up, I'll sweat off twenty pounds."

"That'd be a good start," Sharon says. "I thought you were going to get back to working out."

"I wanted to make sure you were going to see me again."

"What is it with men? You reach a certain age and you plant the La-Z-Boy in front of the TV, and before you know it your six-pack's a gel-pack."

They're back at the Marriott Courtyard in Devon, him having called her as soon as the ballistics test came back on the double shooting at El Campamento. "Thirty-three and thirty-four," he'd said. "Mr. Smith strikes again." He suggested they get together to discuss the case then held his breath, waiting to see if she'd bite. She did, and here they are.

"I guess I could hire one of those twenty-something personal trainers who wears sports bras and the see-my-crotch Lululemon pants."

She punches him. "You'd be dead of a heart attack." He's thinking up a smart comeback, something along the lines of "yeah but it'd be worth it," but he doesn't get it out before she sits up, the covers at her waist.

"This room looks familiar," she says. "Isn't this the one where you brought the strawberries and Reddi-wip that one time?"

"These rooms all look the same to me."

She excuses herself to use the bathroom, and his mind drifts to the case. First Rolli Castillo, lying dead, his face coated with dog urine, then the scene under the bridge, the three dead bodies on the ground, one of which turned out to be a zombie who told him about the tick tock thing.

"You thinking about work?"

"*Tick tock says the clock.*"

She looks at him.

"I think that's what the killer said to the two cousins."

"There was a witness?"

"Sort of. A heroin zombie. I went over to talk to him and he says, 'Tick tock says the clock. Time's up, motherfuck.'"

"And you're thinking he overheard it."

"It was straight through the heart again, with both of them, just like with Rolli."

"Cool as a cucumber, your killer. That's what you're telling me?"

"A real pro," he says, now sitting up next to her. "But dumb enough to use the same gun."

"Maybe it's a sentimental thing, him and the gun."

"I don't think so. Mr. Smith is a gypsy, wandering from hand to hand the past twenty years. Just happens to have found its way to an ace."

"Tick tock says the clock. Time's up motherfuck." She repeats the words a couple times. "Has a nice ring to it. Why do you think he says it?"

"Don't know yet. Maybe to scare 'em. Maybe to gather his nerve."

"Or maybe he just thinks it's cool."

He says he thought of that, too, tells her about *Pulp Fiction* and Samuel L. Jackson.

"So, are you getting anywhere with this case? You and . . . what's your partner's name?"

"Flynn. And no. We canvassed the neighborhood near the bridge and no one saw or heard anything. We even went back to the No-Name, the bar Castillo left when he was whacked, and asked around. We got the same line."

"You expected any different?"

He shakes his head. "Everyone's a Sergeant Schultz: I know nussink!"

"Hardest part of the job."

"Biggest pain in the ass." He exhales. "We'll find something, sooner or later. Something'll break."

"I hope it's sooner. The mayor's fit to be tied. Everyone's saying he's soft on crime, blaming him for the unsolved murders and the opioid problem. His poll numbers are plummeting and he and his chief of staff are scrambling, putting pressure on the commissioner."

"What'd you think of her, the mayor's assistant? You said you met her at that meeting."

"A hot ticket. But has some smarts behind her eyes."

"One of them that's always thinking, eh?"

"*Them?* As in females? Female schemers?"

"As in politicians."

She looks at him, unconvinced. "So, what do you think's behind *my* eyes?"

He takes his time, treads carefully. "More than I'll ever be smart enough to see."

She smiles. "I'll give you an *A* for that answer. Even though I don't think you meant it."

"I did, too, mean it."

"It's true, whether you mean it or not."

"Come here." He reaches for her.

"I'm serious, Ed. You need to do some sit-ups. You need to . . . to . . . ahh."

CHAPTER THIRTY-TWO

RIZZO TAKES OFF his jacket, wraps it around his seatback, sits at his desk. He watches Flynn study an open case file, notices the pile of files on Flynn's desk.

"What are you doing?" he asks Flynn.

Flynn looks up, says, "When you told me about the gun, Mr. Smith, how it's been used in so many different scenarios, I decided to go back and look at the old shootings."

"Yeah? What'd you find?"

Flynn takes a deep breath, then, "Well, starting with Dustin Ross, seems the kid was known to buy opioids in bulk, bring them back to the dorm, and sell them retail."

"I knew that. The brass did, too. But the commissioner told us to keep it under wraps. Said if we leaked it, the public would think we were trashing the kid to divert attention from our unsolved murder rate."

Flynn considers this. "You were right about the liquor store killing, the bank job, pizza delivery man, but . . ."

"But what? Spit it out."

"The bank manager was a wife-abuser. The pizza guy had beaten charges of child molesting on legal technicalities. Twice. The liquor store clerk sold booze to high-school kids, one of which drove drunk and wiped out a family of four. As for the rest of the cases I've read through so far, you have a bunch of drug dealers, a cop-killer, a woman who ran a prostitution ring selling mostly underage girls brought in from the Eastern Block, a lawyer disbarred for stealing his client's money, a doctor sued seven times for botching births, and an investment advisor who cheated dozens of retirees out of their life savings but only served eighteen months."

Rizzo sits back in his chair, studies Flynn. "So, what are you telling me here?"

"Well, I'll keeping looking, just out of curiosity, but so far it seems like everyone killed by that gun was some kind of dirtball."

*   *   *

Rizzo and Leeza sitting at dinner on Wednesday night at Sunset Senior Living. As always, he'd arrived at his mother's apartment at four thirty for the first seating at five sharp. As always, he listened to his mother complain about the staff, the building, the food, the cable TV, for twenty-five minutes before escorting her to the dining room, Leeza zipping along behind her walker, talking the whole way.

When they reached the dining room, Mrs. Cranford was already at Leeza's table, chattering away with three of her friends.

"Look at them, the way they hang on her every word. Sycophants." Leeza glares, then turns away, her nose in the air.

"For Godsakes, Mom, leave it alone."

"She has no idea who she's dealing with."

"I think she does, Mom; you urinated all over her couch."

This brings a smile to Leeza's face.

"It's not funny. And neither was that stunt you pulled with Mrs. Gavin, leaving her in Pottstown."

Another smile.

"You have no idea the strings I had to pull to keep you here after that." The groveling he'd had to do, to the director, two corporate vice presidents, and, of course, Mrs. Gavin's son, another cop whose guts he'd hated since the day they both reported to the Academy. That hurt.

He looks away, takes in the room, pale yellow walls, faded floral curtains, worn carpeting. And the ubiquitous smell of the elderly—a despairing dustiness tinctured with the vague aroma of urine. He hates it, not just the dining room, but the whole place.

Still, he comes. Every Sunday and at least once during the week for dinner. All of the major holidays. And whenever he gets the call from Marie that Leeza has done it again.

"You hardly touched your plate," he says.

"You really expect me to eat this? How much of that meatloaf do you think is meat?"

"Eat it with the gravy."

"Gravy. Ha!"

He sighs.

"Your father should count his lucky stars he died young, never had to come to a dump like this. He ate like a king! Thanks to me."

"Here we go."

*   *   *

Nick Loughead lumbers up the stairs to his second-floor office after a tough day in court, his client having been convicted of possession with intent to sell and carted back to county lockup, where he'd been held for six months awaiting trial. There was no defense, but the client wanted his day in court, so Nick had gone through the motions for two days, pointlessly attacking the prosecutor and cops, even the judge at one point, and giving an impassioned closing argument, all to impress his client with how aggressive he was so that the client wouldn't fault him for the inevitable verdict.

He tosses his leather briefcase onto a chair, sits behind his desk, loosens his tie.

He leans forward and opens the mail left by his secretary. Envelopes from judges, court clerks, and opposing counsel containing all manner of tedious briefs, motions, orders, and notices. Bills from PECO, Comcast, Office Max. Tons of junk mail, mostly law-related, soliciting him for CLE courses, life insurance for lawyers, political contributions, charitable contributions. And, finally, his weekly envelope from the city department of Licenses & Inspections, which, as always, he throws away without opening, L&I being the laziest and therefore least fearsome department in all of city government.

He sorts the mail into piles, then sits back and practices his breathing. Deep breath in, hold for ten, exhale, hold for ten, repeat ten times.

It doesn't work. He's still stressed about the killer, worried the man will come looking for him, press him for money. He's spoken to his uncle Deke three times since the botched hit, each conversation leaving him more concerned than the last.

But tonight, he has the chance to fix the problem. He's meeting with Maleena Rosen, the very unhappy wife of millionaire M.D. Hal Rosen, soon to be broke and playing doctor with tattooed gangbangers in Graterford Prison. Maleena who'd once confided to him that she'd strong-armed her husband to take out five million dollars of life insurance.

He looks at his watch, sees it's getting close to the time he has to meet Maleena at the hotel, and calls an Uber.

He enters the bar to find Maleena waiting for him inside. She tells him she's starving and they decide to walk across the lobby to the restaurant. They sit and order some drinks, and he starts in.

"I've been worried about you."

"You've been worried."

"How are you going to make ends meet when Hal goes upstate?"

"I don't know. He says the government's going to shut down the clinics any day now."

"I read that. You think Hal has money stashed away?"

"He says only a little, enough that his accountant can send me a monthly allowance."

"Allowance? How much?"

"I'm going to have to move. Get a one-bedroom somewhere. Probably have to go back to teaching Pilates. Makes me sick to think about it."

"It doesn't seem right. All you did for Hal. Now he leaves you high and dry." He studies her face, spots the fear, and the anger. Lots of anger. Good.

"You can't even imagine some of the freaky things he had me do. And I know he was stepping out."

"I remember. You told me he tried to hide it at first, but after a couple years he didn't even care that you knew."

Her lip starts to quiver.

"That's the only reason you hooked up with me, because Hal did it first," he says, trying not to choke. He has no doubt he was only one in a long line of Maleena's extramarital partners.

"I wanted to be loyal." She sniffles.

Their entrées arrive, and they eat in silence, until he says, "What if there was a way for you not to lose everything? A way you could keep the house in Gladwyne, not have to go back to work?"

She puts down her fork, leans back, eyes now wary, but listening.

"Are you sure about the money? Doesn't Hal have some kind of asset you could sell, cash in on, to provide for yourself?"

"I don't know what. He's told me the government's going to take everything; it's part of the plea deal."

"I can't believe he didn't go to bat for you, didn't insist on holding something back, to take care of you."

Maleena's face hardens, and it's clear to him that she can't believe it, either.

He waits for the anger to mushroom inside her, then, "Does Hal still have that life insurance policy?"

Her eyes go blank. Then she frowns. "What are you saying? That something bad should happen to my husband?"

He doesn't answer.

"I can't agree to something like that."

He says nothing.

"What kind of person am I that you should even suggest such a thing?"

He just breathes.

"He's been terrible to me, awful, but I mean, I could never . . ." Her voice trails off.

He nods.

After a while, she picks up her fork, takes a bite of Dover sole. She chews daintily, takes a sip of sauvignon blanc.

He watches her enjoying the haute cuisine, the expensive surroundings. Every now and then she glances at her Cartier wristwatch, not for the time, but because she likes wearing something so expensive.

"He could have at least bargained to keep the beach house," she says.

He fills his eyes with sympathy.

"A couple of the cars."

He sighs.

After a while, Maleena says, "The policy is for five million."

He nods his head slowly.

"I wouldn't want him to suffer," Maleena says.

"Of course not. You're a good person."

CHAPTER THIRTY-THREE

A WEEK AFTER the killing under the bridge, Remi's at the Double Eagle Indoor Firing Range. It's a modern facility, twenty-five-yard shooting lanes, concrete flooring, cinderblock walls, electric target retrieval system, armor-plated shooting stalls.

Remi lifts the gun off the counter, extends his arms, and fires. Pop, pop, pop, pop, pop, pop. Six shots, smooth as silk.

He lays the six-shooter on the counter, barrel facing downrange, then reaches up for the button to bring the target back. It stops and he quietly curses. Not a single hole in the target. Again.

This is the third time he's brought the gun to the firing range. He was going to throw the gun in the river—that's why he took it from Virgil's car. But he'd come to figure it didn't matter how many deaths the gun had on it if he was caught. One or three, he'd go away for life—what was left of it. And the truth is he's come to feel an affinity for the weapon, like he and the gun are in this together now. Partners.

It started the Saturday after the double-homicide. Kayla was out with her friends, and he was sitting in his chair watching the ball game. After a while, he caught himself rubbing his right hand. It didn't hurt, exactly. It was more of an itch. Yet not an itch, at least not the kind you scratch. He looked at his hand and didn't find any cuts, or scratches, or even redness. What he did see was that the hand was empty. And just that fast the idea popped into his head that he needed to put something in it and he knew exactly what that something was. So he walked out to his truck and retrieved the gun, took it to his basement, and pretended to practice firing.

The gun felt good in his hand. The weight of it. The heft of the handle as he squeezed it with his palm. The smell of oiled steel.

He decided to take the gun to a firing range. He went online, located one only a few miles away. The front desk guy at the firing range about blew a gasket when Remi opened the bag and he saw that the gun inside was loaded. Thirty tense minutes followed, during which the front desk guy made Remi watch a safety video and then had the range officer personally escort him to the firing stall and repeat everything the video taught about how to safely handle a gun inside the range.

The range officer stood behind him and watched him practice. Three times he emptied the cylinder, and each time he brought the target back to find it untouched, even when the target was out only twenty yards, then fifteen.

"You might want to consider some lessons," the range officer said after the last time.

He saw a couple guys in other stalls smiling, and his face grew hot.

He'd returned to the range twice since—during his lunch hour—and the results were always the same.

Leaving now, he passes the guy up front, hears him mutter to the range officer, "Maybe he should go out to the country, find himself a barn to not hit the side of."

*   *   *

Nick Loughead rushes from City Hall back to his office on 15th Street. His secretary reached him on his cellphone, told him someone from Licenses & Inspections was there, demanding to see him.

"What's this all about?" he says as soon as he reaches his second-floor lobby.

"Mind telling me why you ignored all of our letters?"

Nick studies the man, short, balding, pasty-white. "What letters?"

"The six letters we mailed you over the past two months."

He looks toward his secretary, as though it were her fault, but turns away quickly once he sees the anger in her eyes. They both know she gave him the letters.

"Let's cut to the chase," he tells the guy from L&I. "Why are you here?" He's pretty sure he already knows the answer. Before the karate studio, the first floor was occupied by a restaurant, and it had been impossible to kill off all the cockroaches. At least once a month, his karate tenant, Joe Marazzo, complains about the vermin. Nick gets a pest control company in to carpet bomb, but eventually the relentless bugs return. Karate Joe must've sicked the city on him.

"We're going to do some air testing."

"Air testing?"

"For asbestos."

"There's no asbestos in this building."

"This building's sixty years old. Of course there's asbestos. The question is where and how much. And what type of remediation will be needed."

"Remediation?" This stops him cold. Getting rid of asbestos in a building this size could cost well into the six figures. He knows this because he once brought a lawsuit against the city, alleging asbestos contamination in one of the outlying branches of the library. The city closed the building down rather than pay to remove the toxic insulation.

He starts to hyperventilate, until he remembers who he's dealing with. "Let's go into my private office, talk this over."

Once they're both seated, he smiles and says, "Look. How about I just pay a . . . a . . . fine, and you and I make this all go away."

The inspector glares at him.

"You know, a private fine. Off the books."

The inspector stands. "We're done here."

"Wait!" Nick shoots out of his seat.

"I'll bring the testing equipment tomorrow."

"I wasn't serious, about the fine."

"Well, I am serious, about the asbestos."

Nick watches him leave the office, walk through the lobby toward the stairs, getting angrier with each step the guy takes until he can't hold himself back and shouts, "Since when does L&I actually show up and inspect something?"

The inspector turns and smiles. "We're starting with you."

An hour later, he's still at his desk, rummaging through his top right drawer for the Rolaids he always keeps there. The only thing he finds is an empty wrapper. His stomach has been in knots for days. All he can think about is the unpaid hit man, his uncle calling him every day to remind him the guy's getting more pissed off. He'd hoped Maleena would be the answer to his prayers, but he hasn't heard from her since they had dinner.

What a mess he'd gotten himself into. Never again. No more killings.

He hears the phone ring before his secretary shouts through the doorway, "It's Deke, your uncle."

"Tell him I'm in court," he says, just as his burner phone starts ringing. "Wait, hold on," he calls to his secretary. Then, answering the call on his cell, he says, "Maleena?"

"That thing you brought up, with Hal's insurance—how soon are we talking here?"

He smiles, tells her *soon*, and hangs up. Then, to his secretary: "Tell my uncle I'll be with him in a minute."

CHAPTER THIRTY-FOUR

ELEVEN P.M., AND KAYLA is sitting on the front porch waiting for the car. She was supposed to be away at a basketball camp, but two of the girls got caught smoking weed and the coach had the bus take everyone back to the high school to be picked up by their parents. They arrived after eleven and she drove home, having left her car in the school lot. She expected Remi to be home and asleep, but he was neither. Whatever it was he'd been up to, he was at it again.

There was only one thing to do and that was to head straight to Buford's Garage to see if he was working and, if not, to scour the local bars. But if he was working, she wouldn't want him to see her passing by in her car checking up on him. So, she'd called an UberX and waits for it now.

"Finally," she says, seeing the blue Subaru come to a stop in front of her house. She descends the steps, watches the driver get out and open the rear passenger door for her. She studies him from head to foot, satisfying herself he doesn't look like a perv.

"What in the world do you have on your feet?" she says.

He looks down. "Uh, shoes, miss."

"Penny loafers."

"Brand new."

"With actual pennies in. And is that a sweater vest?"

"I like to dress conservatively, miss. I believe it inspires trust."

"What decade are you from?"

This stops him.

"And don't call me *miss*."

He's about to say "of course, miss," but bites his lip. Instead, he nods to the open door.

"I can ride up front. I'm not some millionaire, and this sure isn't a limo."

"I wouldn't feel right about that." He waves her into the back and she takes her seat, lets him close the door behind her.

"I know I typed in an address in Haverford when I called for you, but we're going somewhere else."

"Uh, I don't know if I can do that. Uber has a very strict policy about taking passengers to the address they've typed into the app. I don't want to get myself into a pickle."

"A what? Listen, I've been taking care of my dad for four years, and he's never gotten into one bit of trouble. Now, all of a sudden, he's out late, comes home with booze on his breath, and some guy supposedly from his past who I never heard of shows up. He's up to something, and I'm going to find out what it is."

The driver stares ahead but doesn't answer.

"Just think of it as an adventure," she says.

She sees him smile.

"Oh, I love adventures," he says.

"That's what I want to hear."

"Where to, then?"

"You know where Buford's Garage is?"

He tilts his head, gives her a weird look in the rearview mirror. "I think so."

She waits a moment, then, "What are you waiting for?"

It only takes a few minutes to get close, and as soon as they do, Kayla spots her father's F-150 leaving the compound and heading toward Lansdowne Avenue.

"Follow that truck," she says and, again, sees him give her that strange look.

* * *

Remi pulls the F-150 out of the compound, on his way to the big house in Gladwyne with the long driveway. Deke laid out the plan for him earlier that day. He's to make his way down the driveway, park in front of the three-car garage, wait for the drug doctor to show, and shoot him.

"He'll probably get out and start cursing at you for being in his driveway. He's a real SOB, according to my guy," Deke had explained earlier.

"Yeah? How's your guy know that?" Remi questioned.

"From the wife."

"Uh-huh. And where's she going to be through all this?"

"She's conveniently on an overnight trip to New York. That's how she knows he'll be out late. Whenever she goes away, he steps out. Never sleeps over, though. Always comes back after midnight."

"How's she know that if she's not there?"

"PI she hired told her."

Remi stared at Deke, who said, "Anything else?"

"You know what else."

"Oh, right," he said, taking the fat envelope from his drawer and sliding it across the desk. "It's all there. Up front. Seventy-five K. Just like you said."

Remi opened the envelope, checked the contents.

"My guy said he busted a gut getting her to come up with the money. Told me it's all she has until the insurance pays off."

Pretending not to hear him, Remi stuffed the envelope into a canvas bag he'd brought. He stashed the bag into his truck-bed toolbox, with the money from the first job, until he can figure out what to do with it so that when he passes, it will show up for Kayla from some source that makes it look legitimate.

Now in his truck heading north on Lansdowne Avenue, Remi thinks back on the conversation with Deke, wondering how much the old man and his guy are going to get on the back end, deciding he didn't care now that he has the seventy-five K. He reaches over to turn up the radio when he sees it in his rearview—the blue Subaru.

"What the . . . ?"

He picks up his cell, punches in Deke's number. It takes a while for the old man to answer. As soon as he does, Remi starts in on him: "The hell's going on, Deke?"

"Huh? What?"

"You got that guy following me."

"What guy?"

"The Uber kid. Virgil."

"I don't have anyone following you, man."

"He's right behind me. Don't deny it."

"But . . ."

"I told you that kid gave me a bad feeling, and I didn't want to work with him no more. I can drive myself."

"And I told you I didn't give a shit whether you have him drive you or not."

"So why is he following me?"

"I. Don't. Know."

"I'll call off this job right now—"

"No! Don't do that. Look, I'll call my guy and see if he knows what's going on."

"You got five minutes." He hangs up, glances into his mirror, and sees the Subaru, thinking the kid might be a good driver but he's terrible at tailing someone, making it so obvious. He glances back and spots a shadow in the rear seat. The kid isn't alone. He's got a passenger.

"Son-of-a-bitch." He's being set up. He does the doctor then he gets whacked. "Not if I can help it."

He turns off the road, races into a development under construction, down a street leading to a cul-de-sac where there are no houses yet. He figures if they get close, he'll screech to a halt, get out firing, hit the one in the back seat first, the shooter. Then go for the kid, which he hates to do because even though there's something creepy about him, he's still just a kid, and very polite.

But they don't follow, which means he's lost them, so he turns back in the direction he came from. A series of twists and turns takes him home, and he pulls into the driveway just as Deke calls him back.

"I just got off the phone with my guy. He swears he has no idea why the kid would be following you."

"To take me off the board is why."

"What're you talking about?"

"The kid's driving another shooter. I saw him in the back seat. *Your guy* was going to let me finish the doctor, then he was going to take me out."

"Why would he do that? He already paid you. A hundred percent up front. Seventy-five grand in your pocket, and no back end for him to fork over. Which, I shouldn't have to remind you, was almost a deal-breaker."

"Well, I got news for you and your guy: me being followed *is* a deal-breaker." He hangs up.

He sits in the truck, his heart racing. He's going to have to do something about this.

Getting out of the truck, he tucks the gun into the back of his pants. He enters the house, surprised he left the living room light on. In the kitchen, he pulls a beer from the fridge, pops the top, and heads out to the porch to figure out what to do.

As soon as he opens the door, he sees the blue Subaru come to a stop. He throws down the beer and reaches around his back for the gun, the plan being to spray the car as soon as he pulls the gun around to his front. Just as he grabs the handle, the rear door to the Subaru opens and Kayla jumps out. His knees buckle and it's everything he can do to keep standing.

"Girl! *What the hell?*"

Watching her approach, he sees the determination in her face turn to confusion.

"Remi? What's wrong? Why did you throw down your beer?"

"I . . . nothing . . . it's just . . . I thought you was going to be away."

"It got all messed up. Kids were caught getting high and the coaches made us come back."

He feels faint, and sweaty, but keeps himself together, trying not to worry her. It doesn't work.

"You don't look right. You should sit down."

He nods and backs up the stairs, sits down, keeping the pistol out of her line of sight.

"Who's that?" he says, nodding toward Virgil, now walking toward them.

"Oh, this is Virgil . . . uh, my friend Christy's brother."

He stares, not liking how easily the lie slides off her tongue. A teenager thing, he figures.

"A little late to be out, isn't it?"

Virgil pipes in, "We were just getting some ice cream, sir."

"Did I ask you?"

Virgil lowers his head, a scolded puppy. "I apologize, sir."

"Kayla, honey, why don't you go inside. I'll walk your, uh, friend here to his car."

She protests that it's not necessary, but he stays firm and in she goes. He listens through the door, hears her go upstairs and close her door.

"Come on," he says, leading Virgil across the lawn to the Subaru.

When they get to the driver's door, Virgil says, "I hate to say it, sir, but she wasn't being truthful. And I made up the thing about the ice cream."

"No kidding. I saw you following me. But I didn't know it was her in the car. I figured you had a shooter planning to finish me once I done the doctor."

Looking hurt, Virgil doesn't answer.

"What's really going on?"

"She's on to you, sir. She knows you're up to something. She just doesn't know what."

"You're telling me she did the app thing for Uber and by sheer luck the driver she got was you?"

"It's a crazy world we live in, sir."

"What a nightmare. You know what would have happened if you'd 'a caught up to me?"

"I have a pretty good idea, sir. That's why I made sure you lost us."

They stand facing each other for a long moment, until Remi tells him to be on his way. Virgil starts to climb in the car, but stops and looks back.

"You mind if I ask you why you didn't allow me to drive you to your . . . assignment? I'm assuming you put the kibosh on me, with my boss."

Kibosh? "It's nothing personal against you, son, me deciding to drive myself. It's just, I don't think a good kid like you should be dragged into something like what I been doing."

"You're very kind, sir. And you're raising a fine young woman! You should be proud."

He exhales and waves Virgil off, watching the car disappear around a corner. Looking up at the house, he sees Kayla duck away from the second-floor dormer. She'd been watching him through the window.

This was too close of a call, he decides. Way too close. He'll make good on the doctor and that'll be it. He's done. More money for Kayla would be nice, but not if the price is him getting caught and her knowing what he's been doing. Or worse, something terrible happening to her, like it almost did tonight.

CHAPTER THIRTY-FIVE

HE'S STILL ON the porch when his cellphone rings. It's Deke, all worked up.

"Goddamnit, Remi. Where are you?"

Before he has a chance to answer, Deke starts up again.

"I just got off the phone with my guy who just got off the phone with that Uber kid. He says the kid wasn't following you at all. He was taking some girl home from a party and you pulled out ahead of him. He was behind you only for a little bit. You turned off the road he was on and that was it, last he saw of you."

He chews on the fact that Virgil lied for him. Lied to his boss, most likely being one and the same as Deke's so-called *guy*.

"You're giving me an ulcer, Remi. You know that?"

"Is that McClaren still scheduled to come in tomorrow?" The bright orange 650-S has been in a couple times. It's owned by a girl, Zelda, a former Delilah's dancer who struck it rich by landing one of those internet millionaire types, a thirty-year-old who supposedly found a way to make money on the web nobody ever thought of before. Fat guy, pockmarked face, never been with a girl before Zelda, or so she'd told Remi the last time she brought in the car. She's a hoot, always makes him laugh, and he could use a good laugh about now.

"McClaren? Who gives a f—"

"Calm down. Tell your guy I'll get the job done tomorrow or the next day. Just get me the address of where he'll be and when'd be the best time to catch him."

He hears Deke exhale in relief on the other end.

"But this is the last time, you hear me? No more of this." He can hear Deke winding up to argue with him, so he hangs up.

*   *   *

On the other side of the tracks, in Bryn Mawr, Nick Loughead paces the carpeted floor of his basement family room, worried Amy will realize he's out of bed and come bother him before he can get this mess ironed out. How would he explain his burner phone?

He just got off the phone with his uncle, relaying what he'd been told by Virgil. Thinking about that kid makes him shiver. Over the course of his career, he'd represented every type of violent offender, from dead-eyed Mafia dons who planned their hits with cool dispassion to crazed killers barely able to contain their zeal for blood. But he'd never met anyone who curdled his own blood like Virgil. Jesus, the things that kid was capable of. So God-awful, the church leadership in Utah banished him from the religion and the state itself. Sent the boy packing to Philadelphia to live with a distant relative, who happened to be one of Nick's clients. A client who owed him big-time.

The cell rings, and he answers without looking to see who it is.

"You shit-head!"

"Maleena, I—"

"It's almost two in the morning and that son-of-a-bitch is still alive."

"Not on the phone!"

"He had the nerve to call me from the house, bitching about how I'd left my clothes laying all over the bedroom."

"Look, there's nothing to worry about."

"I want my hundred grand back. That's all the money I had—"

"And you'll get it all back, fifty-fold, I promise."

"You promised it would be done tonight."

"It won't be tonight, but it will get done. The carpets will all be cleaned. It'll be like you never had a water leak."

"Oh, stop with the fucking code, Nick. You think the FBI won't know what we're talking about if they're listening in?"

She's right, of course. If law enforcement is eavesdropping, he's dead in the water. "Maleena, please. There was just a miscommunication about timing. Everything is still a go."

"It better be. I just put down a deposit on a three-bedroom at the Rittenhouse."

He wants to ask how she paid the down money if the 100K was all she had, but he doesn't. Instead, he decides to go in another direction, talk about something that'll make her smile. "That was nice the other day, when we got together, wasn't it? After we ate."

"Oh, give me a break."

The line goes dead.

He slips the burner into his blue and gold Ralph Lauren robe, a Christmas present from Amy. His chest feels tight and he presses his hand to his heart, starts taking slow breaths. So much stress. So unfair. You try thinking out of the box just once and the world comes after you. Well, no more. From now on, he's just going to mind his business of holding hands with the city's lowlifes, keep them company down the yellow brick road to prison.

CHAPTER THIRTY-SIX

TWO NIGHTS AFTER the aborted attempt on Doctor Hal, Remi parks the rental car behind one of the drug doc's clinics. It's close to seven p.m., about an hour after closing, but Remi knows Rosen is there, because Deke told him he'd be there and because Remi saw Hal's car in the front lot. A gold Lexus with a "Drugdoc" vanity plate.

Deke also told him there were no surveillance cameras on or inside the building, saying his guy told him the place had cameras when the doc bought it four years ago, but he'd had them taken down, given the nature of his business and clientele. Still, it was early, so Remi made sure not to come in his own truck, opting instead to drive a generic four-door Chevy sedan that he'd leased from Budget. For insurance, he replaced the car's plate with one he'd gotten off a junker. He'd switch back the plates before he returned the car.

The building is a one-story cinderblock structure with a metal security door in back. He turns the knob and finds it open, thanks to Doctor Hal's wife having come to visit him just before closing.

Eleven quiet steps down the hall and a quick turn to the right and he's in the doorway of the big man's office. Sitting behind a giant wooden desk, Harold Rosen doesn't see him standing there because his head is back and his eyes are closed. He has an odd expression on his face, Remi placing it somewhere between a trance and the daze of someone in the throes of religious reverie.

Remi clears his throat and the doctor's eyes shoot open. "Who the hell—" He cuts himself short when he sees the gun.

"Tick tock says the clock. Time's up, motherfuck."

He says the words.

He pulls the trigger.

The bullet punches Harold Rosen against the seatback. After a moment, his shoulders slump, but he remains seated behind his desk, head back, eyes and mouth open.

He lowers the gun to his side, watches the crimson stain spread like ink across the drug doctor's white pinpoint oxford.

He turns and leaves.

From beneath the desk, a gagging sound. A muffled cry.

*　*　*

"You're disgusting," Captain Sharon Walker says into her cellphone as she smiles and twirls a lock of her long red hair, driving home for another agonizingly dull night with her husband, Marvin.

On the other end of the phone, Ed Rizzo is about to say something even more racy when the phone on his desk rings. "Damn. Hold on," he says, picking up the phone. A minute later, he's back on with Sharon. "I gotta go. Dispatch just relayed a 911 call from a drug detox clinic in Kensington. A dead doctor, shot once through the heart, or that's how it looks to the patrolman called to the scene."

"You thinking it's them? Your killer and Mr. Smith?"

"We'll know soon enough. Why don't you meet me there?"

"Me? What about your partner?"

"Flynn's on vacation. Disneyland with the wife and kids. But even if he wasn't, it still might help for you to be there."

"Why's that?"

"There's a witness. A woman. She might be more open with you than me."

"How d'you figure?"

"I'll explain when you get there."

"Sorry, I don't do crime scene."

"I understand. You're in a hurry to get home."

She pauses. "I'll be there in thirty."

He laughs as she hangs up.

Half an hour later, Rizzo leads Sharon from her car toward the front door.

"So tell me about the witness, the woman. What does she say the killer looks like? And why didn't he shoot her when she screamed? I assume she screamed when she saw him."

"She didn't see the killer, only heard him. And she couldn't scream; her mouth was full."

"Why are you smiling?"

"She was under the desk."

Sharon furrows, then unfurrows, her brow. "You must be kidding me."

"Nope. Nurse Debbie was polishing the doc's knob."

Sharon stops. "That's why you wanted me here? Because she was giving him a blow job and you thought it'd be funny to bring me into it?"

He winces. "Wow, saying it out loud, it doesn't seem like it was such a good idea."

"Idiot." She turns and strides into the building.

He follows her and, once inside, leads her to a small kitchenette. The nurse—Debbie, her name tag says—is sitting at the table, seeming to Rizzo like she's about to throw up any minute.

Rizzo remains standing while Sharon takes a seat across the table from the nurse, reaches out, touches her hand.

"You okay?"

"This is awful."

"You want some water?"

"I already had some."

To wash out your mouth? It takes an act of will for Sharon not to say it out loud.

"Tell me what happened."

"It's not like . . . we were seeing each other. Dating, you know."

"He was married," Rizzo says, recoiling when he sees the daggers in the nurse's eyes.

"To that whore. Maleena."

Rizzo and Sharon exchange glances.

"When you're ready," Sharon says.

"I already told him," Debbie says, nodding toward Rizzo. "How many times do I have to embarrass myself?"

"Nothing to be embarrassed about. I'm a police officer, this is an investigation, that's all. No judgments here."

Nurse Debbie takes some time to gather herself. Then, "We were being romantic. Me and Hal. I was under the desk. All of a sudden, Hal says something like there's someone else in the room. Next thing I know I hear a gunshot and Hal's body, like, jolts. I freeze. And . . . and . . ."

"You told me you heard the guy, the shooter, say something," Rizzo says.

"It was creepy. He said 'tick tock' and 'time was up' and then he swore."

"Tick tock says the clock? Time's up, motherfuck?"

"That's it!"

"What did his voice sound like?" asks Sharon. "Could you tell if he was young? Old?"

She thinks on it, then, "I think he was older, but not real old. His voice was gravelly. But not deep."

Rizzo nods slowly. "Did he rush through the words? Blurt 'em out fast?"

"No, he said them slow. Like he was enjoying the words. Savoring them, like when you chew something that tastes good. The way he said it, it sounded . . . kind of cool."

Debbie sits up, looks at Rizzo. "Wait a minute. How did you know what he said? He's done it before? How many others? How long's he been out there? Why haven't we heard about this?" She's good and angry now.

"Sometimes we have to hold stuff back," Rizzo says. "For the public's protection."

"Bullshit. You cops hid it because it'd make you look bad if there was a serial killer out there and you couldn't catch him."

"Now, there's no reason to believe he's a serial killer, miss—"

"Really? *Tick tock says the clock* and you don't think he's a psycho?"

Sharon signals Rizzo to leave so she can calm the woman down. After a while, she joins him in the lobby. "She'll come to the station tomorrow, give a formal statement. I asked her to keep the tick tock thing to herself, but I don't think she will. This is going to come out and—"

"And we're going to be in the middle of a shitstorm."

She shakes her head, looks at her watch.

"You want to grab a drink?" he asks.

"Forget it."

He starts to walk away. "Say hi to Marv for me."

"Maybe just one."

CHAPTER THIRTY-SEVEN

GOING ON NINE THIRTY and Remi is sitting in his truck. He'd parked in the driveway, intending to pull the gun from the glove compartment and stow it in the truck-bed toolbox. He's been holding it for a while, liking the feel of the handle against his palm, the click the trigger makes when he pulls it back, the gun-oil smell, it seeming almost a part of him now. Like the words.

"Tick tock says the clock." The words roll off his tongue, liquid gold sliding smoothly down a shoot. "Time's up, motherfuck."

His mind's eye sees the fat drug doctor hear the words, not comprehending at first, then get it the same instant he pulls the trigger. The benefactor supposed to be helping people beat their addictions but really just raking in big bucks making them worse. Until he comes along and says the words and pulls the trigger, and man how good it felt.

"Remi!"

A scream and a shout, and he's pulled from his reverie by Kayla now standing by the truck.

"What are you doing with, with . . . *that*?"

Climbing out of the truck now, wondering where the time went. He'd had it all planned out, to get home by eight thirty and be in the house long before Kayla got home around ten from movie night with her girlfriends. Had he been sitting in the truck for more than an hour?

Seeing the fear in her eyes, he says, "Now, it's nothing for you to be worried about. I just thought maybe now that I'm getting up in years and not as strong as I once was, we should have a little protection—"

"Protection from what?"

"Well—"

"Put that gun down! Stop waving it around."

He looks down at the revolver, still in his hand, horrified that he's holding it with Kayla standing not ten feet away. He quickly turns and jumps onto the back of the truck, opens the box and puts the gun inside, closes the lid, and secures it with the padlock.

"See now," he says, approaching her. "All locked up, safe and sound."

She stares at him, her eyes wide, then turns and rushes into the house.

He lowers his head, thinking he can't believe he'd done that— let her see the gun. *Held it out in front of her, loaded!*

"Jesus." What was he thinking? And what was that strange reverie he'd felt when he'd been in the truck playing with the gun? A high is what it felt like. A trance even, that robbed him of his sense of time, made him blind to Kayla's headlights when she pulled up behind him in the driveway.

"No more of this shit," he says. He's done with all of it. The gun, the shootings, even the money. Can't take a chance of losing himself in that pistol again and winding up shooting Kayla by accident. And even if that didn't happen, he was still pushing his luck with the law. Sooner or later he'd make a mistake and get caught. What good would it do Kayla to get an Ivy League education if she found out her dad was a hired gun? No good at all. Butch Kane was right about that.

No, that gun was going in the river, just like he'd planned. Then would come the hard part. He'd have to sit Kayla down and have the talk, tell her how sick he was. Tell her he wasn't going to be at college graduation—maybe not even last the summer, the way Chuckie Paxton told it. He was hoping to save that for after she turned eighteen, which is right around the corner.

But waiting to tell her is dangerous. If he keeled before she'd had at least some time to steel herself, it could throw her, throw her bad. Maybe even mess her up enough she'd decide to put off college for a semester. And then another semester, and another. And before she'd know it her ship would've sailed.

He shakes his head. Enough of this dark conjuring. He takes a deep breath and climbs the steps into the house, calling her name.

She doesn't answer, so he walks upstairs to her room. He eases open the door, finding her sitting on the bed, arms wrapped around her bent knees. Waiting for him.

"You're scaring me," she says.

He walks to the bed, sits. "There's no reason for you to be upset."

"You have a *gun*. Don't tell me not to be upset."

"Now—"

"Why do you need a gun? Where did you get it?"

"I bought it, from a store. For protection, like I said."

"You're coming home drunk, keeping late hours, driving to who knows where, and now you have a gun."

"What're you talking about? I wasn't drunk that time. And what's this about late hours and driving around?"

"You always get home before seven. But tonight, it's ten—and two days ago—you didn't leave work until almost eleven thirty.

You drove up Lansdowne Avenue, then all of a sudden turned around and came back home. Don't deny it. I saw you."

"You were following me?"

"Yes, and obviously I had every right to." She pauses, then, "Did you know it was me in that car? Is that why you turned around?"

"I never even saw you. I was just wired from working and decided to take a drive is all," he says, the lies gurgling up his throat like vomit, feeling hot and tasting awful. He's never lied to her before all this trouble he'd gotten himself twisted up in.

"You were talking to him for a long time."

He tilts his head.

"The Uber driver. Virgil. I saw you both from my window. It almost seemed like you knew him."

"How would I know an Uber driver?"

"A good question. You want to answer it?"

He stands. "Now you're just bein' paranoid. Seeing things that ain't there."

"There's nothing wrong with my vision."

He looks at her for a long minute.

"I want you to get rid of that gun. Tomorrow."

Tick tock says the clock. Times up—

"Do you hear me?"

"I already made up my mind to do just that."

She studies him and her eyes well up. "I can't believe you brought a gun home. And waved it in my face."

His shoulders sag, his neck bows. *I can't believe it, either, baby.* "Tomorrow, I'm done with it."

CHAPTER THIRTY-EIGHT

NICK SITTING AT his desk, talking to Alvin Richmond, an old law school classmate, both of them yucking it up. Their law school reunion is coming up, and Alvin, now living in Wyoming, called out of the blue.

"So how's the practice of law in Wyoming?" asks Nick.

"I have a guy vacationing on a dude ranch, a New Yorker, sells bonds or something, slipped on horse shit and ruptured a disc in his back. So I wait until he has his surgery then file suit. The ranch offers 100K. I tell the guy that's a fair amount, he should take it. He spits in my face over the phone. Says his case would get two million in Manhattan."

"Two million?"

"I told him the whole ranch is only worth twice that. He told me to demand it anyway, see what they said."

"What did they say?"

Alvin chuckles. "The rancher said they saved the shit the guy slipped on, as evidence. 'Tell your client we'll give him half a million, but he has to come back to the ranch and eat it.'"

"Yeah? What'd he say?"

"The rancher said, he said, 'All of it?'"

"No way."

"I swear to god."

They laugh.

"Oh, man, it's good to talk to you," Alvin says. "I can't believe how long it's been."

They sigh, and Nick shares some amusing tales about representing drug dealers and sex offenders, judiciously omitting his murder-for-hire racket.

Alvin listens enviously, then says, "You remember that tall brunette you were boning? Lauren? You know whether she'll be at the reunion?"

Nick smiles. "No, but I'll ask her, next time I'm riding her like a bronco at your client's dude ranch."

"You're still nailing that? Oh, man, you're killing me."

"Ah," Nick says, shrugging it off. "It's getting old. I'm thinking of letting go of her."

"Really?" Alvin says. "Before or after the reunion?"

"You're still a hound dog yourself, I see."

Nick leans his head back for a good belly laugh, but before he can get it out, he's interrupted by a loud knock.

"I'm on the phone," he complains through the door.

"You need to get out here," his secretary snaps back.

"Pain in the . . ." Nick shakes his head, apologizes to Alvin before hanging up.

He opens his office door and is about to snipe at his secretary when he spots the short little baldy in the gray suit. The guy from L&I.

Nick sees the smile spread across the man's face, as he walks toward him.

"Mr. Loughead. I'm afraid I have some bad news."

"Asbestos?" Nick's heart sinks.

"Oh yes, and plenty of it. But that's not your real problem."

Nick stares.

"Stachybotrys chartarum. Ever hear of that?"

"Staki—"

"Black mold."

Nick rubs his throat.

"Produces trichothecene mycotoxins, which are neurotoxic. Tell me, do you ever experience confusion or brain fog? Difficulty concentrating? How about tingling, trembling, or shaking?"

Nick glances at his secretary, whose eyes are wide. She starts rubbing her hands and fingers.

"This is ridiculous. I've never felt any of that. There's no mold in this building."

"I assure you, there is. And it's especially concentrated in the locker room and karate gym downstairs. They'll have to be closed off, of course. And the parents notified to have their children tested."

Nick sways. He carries minimal personal injury insurance, and if he alerts the karate kids' parents about the mold, he'll be hit with a hundred lawsuits by the end of next week.

"There has to be something I can do," he says, his voice weak.

"Oh, there is, absolutely. It'll require you to demo the inside of the building down to the brick, of course, given the levels we found. But the shell should survive totally intact. You and your tenant can both be back in the building inside of a year, if you find a good contractor."

"A good contractor?" *As if there were such a thing.*

"Come on, don't be so upset. A smart guy like you, I'm sure you have this building insured to the hilt."

Nick moans.

"Here you go." The little L&I guy hands Nick a pile of papers. "These are our findings. And the notice to evacuate."

"How long—"

"Tomorrow should be fine, for you. The gym will have to be closed immediately, as I'm sure you'll understand."

Nick's mind is numb as he watches the man leave, his bald head bobbing with the spring in his step. When the inspector is gone, he turns to his secretary, who is hurriedly shoving her picture frames into her purse.

"You're leaving?"

"My husband and I are trying to get pregnant. I may already be pregnant. You better pray my baby doesn't have a birth defect, that's all I can say."

She turns and bolts for the stairs to the ground level one floor below. Nick hears Joe Marazzo, on his way in, say hello to her. They talk for a moment, too low for Nick to make out what they're saying, until Marazzo's voice explodes in expletives.

Nick stands frozen in place as Joe bounds the stairs two at a time, no easy task for such a big man, Nick thinks, even if he is a fourth-degree black belt.

Nick whimpers. *This is going to hurt.*

CHAPTER THIRTY-NINE

IT'S REMI'S LUNCH HOUR and he's sitting in the robing room, across the desk from Father Kane. He's told the priest about the drug doctor and about Kayla catching him with the gun. The priest shakes his head.

"I'm feeling real sorry," Remi says.

The priest, looking more like Butch, the tough guy, than Lenny, nods once but doesn't answer.

"That's remorse, right? When it hurts?"

"What is it that you're sorry about? Really? That you've killed four men? Or that your daughter caught you with the evidence and made you feel like a shit?"

"I could have killed her. If the gun'd gone off, by accident."

"And the men you killed *not* by accident? How do you feel about them?"

He opens his mouth but doesn't say anything.

"Remi. Look at me. You kill people. For money—"

"For my daughter—"

"It *doesn't matter* what you want the money for. You have made yourself into a cold-blooded murderer."

He drops his head.

"What are you looking for from me?"

"I don't know," Remi says, shaking his head.

"Well, damn it, man, you need to think on it. There's a reason you came here. Maybe you can't feel it yet, but it's inside you. Something that needs letting out, something that needs to be seen and heard and . . . *saved*."

"And you can do that? You can save—"

"Me? No. But you know who can."

He considers what the priest has said, and reaches inward, but can't quite grasp the lump that's been forming inside his chest.

"In the meantime: Stop. Killing. People."

"I'm done with that!" He blurts the words. "Believe me. Enough is enough."

The priest leans back in his chair, extends his hands. "Then give it to me."

"Huh?"

"The gun. Give me the gun."

"Oh. I don't have it with me. I used to keep it in my truck, but I took it to the woods, a place nobody goes, put it under a rock. I'm gonna drive it to the river, next day or two, throw it in."

He means it, too, and it's a good thing he does because other-wise he'd shrivel for sure under the hard look the priest is giving him.

They sit in silence again, until Kane asks him, "Have you told her yet? About your heart?"

He exhales. "I keep thinking about it. But I just can't bring myself to."

"You have to tell her. You know that, right?"

"I'm going to. I am." He pauses, feels the priest's eyes boring into him.

"It's just . . . it's like it's not real, you know. I mean, I heard it from the doctor, and I can still hear him in my head, but nobody else knows—well, you and my lawyer know—but nobody else, especially Kayla. But once she knows, then it'll be something real, between her and me. There all the time."

"You have to stop pretending and face the hard truth. She's going to have to face it, too."

He nods, stands abruptly. "I best get back to work now."

Father Kane walks him to the door. "Listen to me. You can't keep putting things off with your daughter. And you can't keep putting things off with God. Not with your sins, Remi. Not with your heart. The clock is ticking. Your time's almost up. What are you staring at?"

CHAPTER FORTY

ELEVEN TWENTY-FIVE P.M., two nights after the drug doctor killing. Rizzo is asleep on his couch.

The doorbell rings.

He forces himself up and stumbles his way to the door. It's Sharon.

He wipes the haze from his eyes, then, "It's late. You all right?"

She brushes by him, turns around in the middle of the living room. "What's there to drink around here?"

"You like Crown Royal? Maker's Mark?"

"Wow, the good stuff."

He gets a bottle and two glasses, joins her on the couch, and pours. "Here," he says.

He waits. She takes a long swallow. Then another.

"I told Marv I want a divorce."

"Jeez."

"Know what he said? He said, 'Well, we'll have to figure out how to minimize the tax consequences.' Can you believe that? I tell him I'm leaving, and his first thought is our taxes."

"What'd you say?"

"Not so much what I said as what I did."

"Here we go."

"I walloped him on the side of the head, with his shoe."

"Oh boy." He watches her stew. "He call the cops?"

"No. But he was pissed, after I hit him. First time I found a way to get him mad in all the years we've been married."

He places his glass on the coffee table. "You look tired."

"I'm not tired. I'm angry. Really angry. Come on, let's go to bed."

"And they're off."

She stops in her tracks and spins around. "You know I'm carrying, right?"

"Sorry."

* * *

He wakes the next morning to the smell of bacon frying in a pan. He smiles and takes it in; he can't remember the last time someone cooked for him. After a while, he makes his way to the kitchen, leans against the doorjamb.

"Don't say anything smart, or I'll stop right now."

"I wasn't—"

"Yes, you were. I could see it on your face. That smug little smile. You were putting together something along the lines of women belonging in the kitchen. But your brain doesn't work that fast, so you never got it out."

"You got me all wrong," he says, moving to the coffee maker, pouring himself a cup, refilling hers.

He sits at the table and watches her, feeling happy.

Sharon finishes with the bacon and piles it on their plates with the scrambled eggs she'd already cooked. When the toast pops, she adds it to the mix and carries the plates to the table.

They eat for a while, then he says, "I'm glad you're here."

She looks at him for a minute then resumes chewing.

"How about you?" he asks.

She pauses again. "We'll see."

When he's finished, he says, "You have a lawyer?"

"No. It was a spur of the moment kind of thing, me telling Marv I want out. I mean, I've been thinking about it, but . . ."

He nods, and she catches him staring at her.

"And no, it's got nothing to do with you."

"I didn't say it did."

"What, you think you swept me off my feet? Made me lose my senses, I'm so infatuated with you?"

"No, I—"

"If anything, I should be hating you right now."

"Me?"

"You were part of the reason I married him. You were so self-destructive back then, and I got caught up in your vortex. Almost ruined my career. Certainly lost my reputation within our unit. Then even-keeled Marv came along, and he seemed like just the type of guy I needed to get me back on track."

"Back on track," he repeats the words.

"And he was, for a while, good for me, I mean. I was able to refocus. Put my nose to the grindstone, follow the rules, play the politics. Got promoted, and kept on getting promoted. Now I got my captain's bars. And no one can say I didn't earn them," she adds, pointing her fork at him.

"Everyone knows how hard you work," he says, wanting to join in, show his support.

They finish eating and he takes the dishes from the table, loads them into the dishwasher along with the pans while she leaves the kitchen to take a shower. He wipes off the table then moves through the dining room into the living room, where he finds her staring at the TV.

"Uh-oh," he says, reading her face.

"Uh-oh, is right."

He moves up beside her and looks down at the screen, where Nurse Debbie is telling her tale to Channel Six beat reporter Jennifer Yamurra.

"Tick tock, says the clock. Time's up, mother-you-know-what."

"And you said you could hear the killer but not see him?"

"I was . . . hiding in the closet."

The gleam in the reporter's dark eyes tells Rizzo she knows where Debbie was really hiding, and what she was doing there.

"The worst part is the detective who showed up already knew what the killer said. Which means this guy's been killing people all along, and the cops have been covering it up."

Here, Yamurra turns to the camera and says to the anchor, "And isn't that exactly what ballistics is showing?"

Rizzo and Sharon turn to each other and say, "Shit." They know what's coming.

Anchorman Jim, now before the camera, says, "Action News has learned that the gun used to kill Doctor Rosen has been implicated in thirty-four prior homicides, including a shooting earlier this month outside a bar in North Philadelphia and the double-homicide a short time later at El Campamento. And"—here, Jim pauses for dramatic effect—"the killing last year of Drexel engineering student Dustin Ross."

Jimbo pauses, and Rizzo sees the glee glint across his eyes.

"For more on the weapon," the anchorman says, "we turn to Aron Vicarro, standing outside police headquarters. Aron, tell us what you've learned about the gun."

The camera cuts to a well-coiffed young man holding a microphone outside the roundhouse. "It's really quite amazing, Jim. According to our anonymous source inside the police department, the gun has been used in murders going back more than twenty years. It's one of the department's darkest secrets. The police actually have a name for it—"

Sharon moans.

"Mr. Smith."

"We are so screwed," says Rizzo.

CHAPTER FORTY-ONE

LATER THAT SAME morning and Rizzo and Sharon are sitting side by side, across the desk from Police Chief Carl Bolton.

"Thirty-four killings with the same gun? The revolver so well known within the department it has a name? And now it's in the hands of some psycho killer, uttering a couplet before he pulls the trigger?"

"Chief?" Sharon said. "I'm not sure why I've been drawn into this."

The chief sighs, shakes his head.

"I mean, I'm a precinct captain," Sharon continues. "The investigations are for the detectives."

Rizzo turns to her. "Throw me under the bus that fast, eh?" Sounding hurt but smiling inside thinking about her riding him the night before, wearing her captain's hat, her little boobies bouncing up and down.

"No one drew you into this," says the chief. "You showed up at the crime scene, remember? Interviewed the witness."

"I was *asked* to," she says, nodding at Rizzo. "If I'd known about Mr. Smith, I wouldn't have come within a mile of that crime scene."

"The commissioner had me on the hot seat for an hour this morning," Chief Bolton complains.

"As if you've never heard of the gun," Rizzo says to Sharon. "Give me a break."

Rizzo turns back to Bolton, whose face is red turning to purple. "We look like the damned Keystone cops," Bolton says.

"Well, this is Pennsylvania, so technically—"

"Not another word, Rizzo!" The chief, now standing, paces behind his desk, then asks if they have any leads.

"All we got in the Castillo and El Campamento killings were doors slammed in our faces."

Chief Bolton shakes his head. "We're fighting crime with two hands tied behind our backs, the way no one talks to us. It's their neighbors getting killed, their friends and family, but will they point us in the right direction? Not a chance."

"The Rosen murder might be different. This isn't some street peddler got killed. It was a doctor. Dirty as a shit-tick, for sure, but a bigwig."

"Dirty? How?"

"His clinics were fronts. He was selling prescriptions for Suboxone and Klonopin. There's a sealed indictment against him came down a few weeks ago, and his lawyer was ironing out a plea deal for him. A friend in the DA's office shared this with me. On the QT, of course."

"Another secret that everyone knows."

"I didn't know," Sharon says.

Rizzo turns to her, stares. He wants nothing more than to grab her and kiss her as hard as he can. She's that hot. Instead, he turns back to the chief. "I've been trying to talk to the vic's wife but she's putting me off, her maid telling me over the phone she's too upset."

"Over the phone? Go to her house. Bust down the door if you need to. We need a break on this case, and fast."

*   *   *

"You little SOB." Remi striding into Deke's office, arm extended, finger pointed. "You and that Mr. Smith put a needle in my arm." He says the words knowing they're ridiculous; his heart will kill him long before the state could, assuming they caught him, which he doubts they will.

"Now, Remi," Deke says, his own arms extended, trying to waive away Bone's anger. "I told you before I didn't know nothing about that gun."

"The cops, the news, everyone thinking I'm some kind of mass murderer who's been prowling the streets with that revolver going on twenty years."

"I thought you were going to get rid of it and use something else. That's why you took it from the kid."

"I did get rid of it. I buried it where no one can find it. But it's too late now, ain't it?"

He lowers himself onto the chair and Deke sits, too. They stare at each other until he says, "Where you been the past two days?"

"Not feeling well," Deke answers.

"You was hiding from me till the heat died down. Except it's only getting worse, the people wanting the mayor's head, and the commissioner's and the chief's. And all of them pointing at each other and probably having the whole damn force out looking for me."

"Now, I think your own head's running away with itself. This'll die down. It always does. Something bad happens and everyone's up in arms for a week or two, then the world moves on to something else. Some tsunami in Japan or earthquake in China, a hundred thousand dead and the talking heads can't get enough of it. Plus, there's the big transit strike coming up. That'll get people good and pissed and they'll forget all about the Tick Tock killer. You just wait and see."

"Don't you mention the Tick Tock thing. I'm sorry I ever said it."

"How'd you come up with that?"

"I don't want to talk about it."

"Does this mean you're done?"

"Damn right it does. But first I want to know who's the guy been setting this all up."

Deke's eyes darken. "You know I can't tell you about him."

"But I bet he knows who I am. At least that I work for you."

"I never told him that," Deke says, but the delay before he gets it out tells Remi he's lying.

Remi spots the fear dancing in Deke's eyes, telling him Deke knows that he knows Deke's lying.

"I mean it, Remi. He don't know who you are and he can't tell anyone. I'm the only one he knows, so all the risk's on me."

"Until the police put their thumbs to you. Talk to you about metal beds and group showers, and you decide to throw some of the risk my way."

Deke shoots to his feet. "Now that's not fair! I'm not a rat. Never have been and never will be. You got nothing to fear from me."

Remi stands, gives Deke a hard look, then turns and walks out of the office. *Let him spend some long nights awake in his bed. Listening for noises in his house, thinking it might be me.*

* * *

Deke watches Remi leave, then walks to the door and closes it. Back at his desk, he punches the numbers in his cellphone. The line rings and rings, then goes to voicemail.

"We have a problem, damnit. *Call me.*"

He's been trying to get through to his nephew since the story broke about tick tock and Mr. Smith. But Nick the prick isn't picking up. Deke has a good mind to get in his car and drive to Nick's office in Center City. He'd do it, too, except that might make Remi even more suspicious. And there's no way he's paying $34 to park.

Through the glass wall, he watches Remi arrange his tools in preparation to work on a yellow Lamborghini. He knew he could get Remi to do the dirty work. But the man seems to have taken to it just a little too much. The Tick Tock thing proves it. Saying that to a guy right before he whacks him shows that Remi's liking what he's doing. *And now he's pissed off at me, thinks I put him in danger with my contact. Not good.*

"Tick tock says the clock. Time's up, motherfuck." One way or the other, Remi Bone's got to go.

CHAPTER FORTY-TWO

LAUREN GLANCES AT the mayor slumped at his desk, the heels of his hands pressed firmly against his temples. The tumbler of bourbon she poured just a moment ago is empty.

The television, tuned to Fox 29, shows Dilworth Plaza packed with protesters.

"I hate it that they always show up just in time for the six o'clock news," Wallace Brown whines.

The phone rings.

"No more calls!" shouts Brown.

Lauren walks to the desk, picks up the receiver, listens for a moment. Her hand covering the mouthpiece, she turns to the mayor. "I think you should take this. It's Dustin Ross's mother."

"I've already talked to that woman four times in the past two days. And I've spoken six times to that nitwit leader of the El Campamento crowd. You know the last time, he actually threatened me? Said I if didn't clean up the area, he'd bring the zombie apocalypse to the business district, whatever the hell that means."

Lauren stares at him.

"How many times can I say I didn't know anything about Mr. Smith, and that I can't force Conrail to clean up its human shithole?"

Lauren listens, does her best to feign sympathy. When news of Mr. Smith and the Tick Tock killer broke two days ago, the collective consciousness of the city's citizenry seemed to snap. The gun and its bearer came to symbolize City Hall's impotence against both gun violence and the opioid crisis, which became intertwined in the public mind. After forty-eight hours of ceaseless protests, scathing media condemnation, and outright threats, her boss is at his breaking point.

Removing her hand from the mouthpiece, Lauren says, "I'm sorry, Mrs. Ross. He's on the phone with the governor. Mrs. Ross? Mrs. Ross?"

"This is all the cops' fault, you know. When's the last time you think our three-hundred-pound commissioner actually got up from behind his desk and went out to fight crime? *Effing Walrus.*" He thinks for a minute, then says, "I should've joined the protesters the first time they showed up, let the people know exactly where the blame belongs in this mess."

"Mr. Mayor, blaming the police would be a bad move. You don't want them turning their backs on you, like they did with de Blasio in New York. The optics would be terrible."

"That damned word again."

From outside the office, the mayor's secretary buzzes him. He sighs and presses the button. "What?"

"The children's group is here, sir. The Young Leaders Group. For the photo op."

This perks him up. "At least the kids don't hate me."

Yet, thinks Lauren.

"Bring 'em in," he says. Then, to Lauren, "Big smiles."

* * *

Twelve miles north and west, in a large stone home in Gladwyne, Ed Rizzo and Patrick Flynn sit on an impeccably restored Milo Baughman sofa. Across from them, in a checkered cream Annie Selke wing chair, is Maleena Roseman starring as the grieving widow.

"We're very thankful you agreed to see us," Rizzo says. "Though, two days is a long time to wait to speak to the wife in a murder investigation."

"I just couldn't do this any sooner. I was a wreck. A total wreck." Maleena dabs the corner of her eye with a handkerchief. "I still can't believe my Harold is gone."

Your Harold, Rizzo thinks. *And Debbie's Harold.* "I can only imagine how painful this must be for you."

"You don't know the half of it."

"Why don't you share it with me?"

This causes her to stop. She doesn't know how to answer.

"Did your husband have any enemies, Mrs. Roseman? Someone who might want to do him harm?"

"That's impossible. Harold was almost a saint. Helping all those people defeat drug addiction. He won awards."

"Any trouble on the horizon, that you were aware of?" Rizzo asks, trying to find out if she knows about her husband's legal problems—the sealed indictment and his plea deal and imminent incarceration. Maybe Harold was the type to keep it a secret right up until the end. He'd known perps like that, tell their wives, "Come on, let's go for a drive," then pull up outside the prison, say, "I'll see you in five years."

"Trouble?"

Oh yeah, she knew. This Maleena is as good-looking as any woman on network TV, and as bad an actress.

"The news people are saying Harold was shot by the Tick Tock killer. That serial killer you police have known about for years."

Rizzo says, "The muckrakers are selling muck, Mrs. Roseman." He pauses, then says, "Your husband's nurse, Debbie, the one who heard the killer, we know she wasn't married. Do you know whether she had a boyfriend?"

Her eyes narrowing at the mention of the nurse's name, she answers, "I . . . why?"

"Jealousy, a lot of times, is why people get shot in the workplace. Some guy gets wind of something between his spouse or girlfriend and her employer, and shows up with a chip on his shoulder and a gun in his hand."

Rizzo watches Maleena puzzling out which way to go. Should she say the idea is outrageous because her husband was obviously faithful to her, or jump on the jealous boyfriend bandwagon? Or, maybe take another direction.

"I only met her once or twice, that Debbie. But there was something about her I just didn't trust. Is it possible she shot my Harold herself and made up this whole Tick Tock thing?"

Door number three. "No. There was someone else involved. The Tick Tock guy is real."

"Then you did already know about him."

Her voice now spiced with indignation. Not over the top, though, Rizzo thinks. She's getting better with her lines.

"We knew about the gun, not the man. But the good news is that we'll get him this time."

This gives her pause. "How can you be so sure? Your department solves less than 50 percent of murders; everyone knows that."

"That figure's counting drive-bys and gang killings. For something like what happened to your husband, the percentages are much higher."

"Oh," she says, her face losing some color. "Good."

Rizzo stands and walks toward the door, Flynn taking his lead, Maleena, too. When he gets to the threshold, Rizzo turns and puts his hands on her shoulders.

"Rest assured, Mrs. Roseman, I will catch the person responsible for your husband's death. I'll march right into their house, pull out my handcuffs and take them away, and they'll never see the light of day again."

Her face now completely drained of blood, she says, "That's . . . nice."

*　　*　　*

On the way back to the station now, Flynn driving, Rizzo riding shotgun. "You think it was her? That she arranged it?" Flynn says.

"I'm betting there's a fat insurance check in the mail right now."

Flynn glances at him, then turns his eyes back to the road.

"She sells the house for a smaller place, gets a job, I'm wrong. She keeps the house, I'm right."

"But, either way, this was no isolated, random killing," Flynn says.

"It's one guy who did this and the El Campamento job and Rolli Castillo, too. A pro. Not a psycho, even with the tick tock thing."

"A hit man, doing it for money."

"Somehow or other, he gets his hands on Mr. Smith, and they become a pair, like in one of those buddy films. Mel Gibson and Danny Glover. *Lethal Weapon*."

Flynn smiles. "Owen Wilson and Vince Vaughn. *Wedding Crashers*."

"Walter Matthau and Jack Lemon. *Grumpy Old Men*."

"John Cho and Cal Penn. *Harold and Kumar Go to Whitecastle.*"

"You just ruined it."

*　*　*

The next day, three days after the Tick Tock/Mr. Smith story broke, and one day after his confrontation with Deke, Remi sits at the breakfast table, watching Kayla whipping up a healthy egg-white omelet for him.

"I put in some spinach. You want tomatoes or orange peppers?"

"No thank you."

"It's no problem."

"Spinach is fine."

"Tomato probably goes best with the spinach," she says, and pulls a plastic container out of the fridge.

He smiles, loving her. But inside he's torn up. He's got to tell her about his heart. Even without Butch, or Lenny, telling him, he knows it's the right thing to do. But he just can't seem to find a way to broach the subject. What's he going to say, "Hey, honey, if you're thinking about what to get me for Christmas, don't bother"?

He watches her cooking the eggs, loading the toast into the toaster, pouring the orange juice and placing it onto the table, her motions fluid and confident. His Kayla, so sure of herself, a rare thing, he's heard, when it comes to girls her age, supposedly wrestling with insecurities and negative body images.

He sighs, reaches for the newspaper, the front-page headlines still screaming about Mr. Smith and the Tick Tock killer, and folks in the Badlands up in arms about the opioid problem and El Campamento. It's upsetting to him, so he turns the page without reading the articles. He scans the following pages finding little of interest, until he sees it: the picture. Kayla, and half a dozen other kids her age, all smiles, and all of them standing next to *him.*

His heart starts to pound and his stomach churns. He feels short of breath.

"You're in the paper," he says.

"Let me see," she says, moving beside him and studying the photograph.

"What . . . what . . . ?"

"It was the young leadership thing, with the mayor. You knew about that. That was the field trip to the city I told you was coming up."

"You didn't say anything about being with the mayor."

"He was so nice. His whole staff was."

Remi can't pull his eyes from the picture.

"The mayor spent a lot of time with us, asked all our names and where we were from and what our plans were."

"He asked your name? Where you live?"

"He said he would follow us, follow our careers as students. And"—she lowers her voice— "as we were leaving, he held me back, and said he was going to pay special attention to me. He said I reminded him of someone he once knew, and he was sure I would grow up to be very special."

Remi looks up at her, does his best to hide his terror, and the slow boil of his blood.

"Are you okay? What's the matter?"

"Me? Nothing. I'm just hungry is all. Waiting for those eggs."

She looks down at him and smiles. "If I didn't know better, I'd swear you were jealous, of the mayor."

"That's ridiculous," he says, a little too emphatically.

"He is handsome," she says, toying with him. "And very charismatic." She smiles again, then leans in from behind and hugs him, kisses him on the cheek. "But he's not my dad. You are."

*　*　*

At the same time, in Center City, Nick Loughead paces his office. He's not supposed to be there—no one is. L&I's posted a big red placard on the door warning that the building is unsafe for occupancy.

"Screw them," he says to no one.

So far, he's fielded seven calls from angry parents of kids who'd taken karate lessons on the first floor. Asking if there really is a mold problem, demanding to see the test results. Threatening to hire lawyers.

"Screw them, too," he says.

He looks at his watch. He doesn't have to be anywhere until the afternoon, when he's scheduled to make oral argument on a motion to suppress, the evidence at issue being four pounds of marijuana. He has no chance of winning—the pot was in plain view in the back seat of his client's car, pulled over when the client ran a red light. "Idiot."

Under normal circumstances, he wouldn't complain. Idiots keep him in business. Idiots in the form of drug dealers, sex offenders, burglars, arsonists, drunk drivers, wife-beaters, and pornographers—the writhing, slithering, teeming maggotry of bottom-feeding reprobates ceaselessly sucked in, digested, and excreted by the city's criminal justice system.

But these are not normal circumstances. In his quest to better himself, he'd put into motion his own mini Murder Inc., which seems to have accomplished nothing other than to put him under the thumb of his trailer-trash uncle, and, if Deke is right, high up on the shitlist of the whack artist Deke enlisted to do the killing.

That's the bad news. The slightly less bad news is that his building, which represents 90 percent of his worldly wealth, is now worth approximately zero dollars, thanks to a black mold problem so severe it will eventually kill him if the hit man doesn't get pissed off enough to do it first.

He's been racking his brain for days trying to find a way to escape this two-headed hydra and has come up empty. There must be someone out there who's faced a similar situation—a peer in the criminal defense bar, most likely—but it'd be impossible to reach out for advice without exposing himself.

He walks behind his desk and flops into his chair, defeated. He looks around the room, then lifts the remote and turns on his TV.

It opens to a CNN report on the mayor, his travails having gone national. The anchor's eyes glitter as she reads the copy about Wallace Brown's plummeting pole numbers, his once bright political future dimming by the second, thanks to the city's plague of unsolved murders, intractable opioid problem, and the blight in the Badlands symbolized by the heroin zombie-infested, hell-on-earth known as El Campamento.

Behind the anchor is a video showing the mayor fighting his way through an angry crowd of protesters. "You should be protesting down at police headquarters," he shouts, after which a mounted officer relaxes his grip on the reins and the horse's rear haunches bump into the mayor, almost knocking him over.

Nick shakes his head. "That is one desperate man." Maybe the only person in Philadelphia in more trouble than—

Nick bolts up in his chair. "Whoa." Could that be the answer? Wallace Brown has long been known to wheel and deal. A couple of Eagles tickets tossed his way and the Streets Department comes and smooths out those potholes in front of your house. A nice vacation for him and his wife and your company gets awarded a lucrative concession at the airport. Two years ago, it was whispered that a corporate law firm was awarded a big chunk of the city's bond work after its managing partner helped get the mayor's lackwit niece into Yale.

His heart beating a mile a minute, Nick takes some deep breaths, then picks up the phone.

"Lauren? It's me. How about I come and pick you up for lunch?"

"What? Come where?"

"To your office."

"Is this a joke?"

"I can't take you to lunch sometimes?"

"You're married, remember. And I have a reputation to protect."

"We're old friends from law school, going to lunch. Nothing suspicious about that."

"Then why am I feeling suspicious?"

"See you in ten," he says, hanging up before she can shut him down. He leans back in his chair, closes his eyes, sets his mind to working on how he's going to make his play at the mayor's office. Once he's satisfied with his plan, he lets his mind drift to his uncle, and then to the hit man who has a hard-on for him. He smiles. "Tick tock says the clock."

CHAPTER FORTY-THREE

RIZZO AND FLYNN tail Maleena Roseman from the King of Prussia Mall toward her home in Gladwyne. They waited outside Neiman Marcus for almost two hours, watching her hand the car off to the valet and then coming out, loaded down with bags.

"I wonder who she's talking to," says Flynn, spying her on her cellphone, through the rear window of her Bentley Continental.

"Why do women like white cars?" says Rizzo. "I had a sporty car like that, it'd be black."

"That's more a luxury car than what you'd call sporty. A 350Z is sporty. Or a Mustang."

"Nissans and Fords. And we're tailing a Bentley. Were you raised in a trailer? You don't know the difference?"

"We're talking style here, not price."

"She's probably talking to her boyfriend is my guess."

"You think she was stepping out on the doctor?"

"You kidding? That body, those legs. And she's what, in her late twenties? Old Harold was twice her age. And probably three times her weight."

"I wonder how they met."

"How does someone like her ever meet someone like him? They *find* a way, that's how."

"What do you think about all that stuff she came out of the store with?"

"And all from Neiman's. Not a place a girl goes when she thinks she's about to run outta money."

"Unless she's looking to land another fish and thinks she needs a fresh look."

Rizzo nods. "You could be right. But I'm still thinking she's waiting for a big insurance check."

They drive for a while. Rizzo's cellphone rings, and he pulls it out of his jacket. Seeing that the number belongs to Sunset Senior Living, his blood comes to an instant boil. Another call from Marie, about another outrage committed by his mother. "This is getting to be too much, goddamnit," he mutters to Flynn.

He lifts the phone to his ear. "Now what?" he snipes.

A pause at the other end. "I'm sorry, Ed. I'm so sorry."

* * *

Lauren finishes up in the ladies' room and walks down the hall to the mayor's suite. She's not happy at Nick's decision to pay a surprise visit to her workplace. He's up to something, she's sure of it. But what? The few times they'd done nooners, he met her at a hotel. Nick was paranoid that his wife, or one of her friends, or relatives, would see them together in public and rat him out. Although he didn't come out and say it, she'd read between the lines that none of Amy's friends or family members like him. There has to be a reason he's willing to risk exposure by visiting her at work and taking her to lunch.

She enters the outer office, expecting to see Nick waiting on the couch. He's not there and for a second she feels a sense of relief, thinking maybe he's changed his mind. But then she glances at the mayor's secretary, who nods toward the open door to the mayor's office. *Oh no!*

With a Herculean effort, she resists the urge to lunge toward the doorway. Instead, she calmly walks into the mayor's office, where she finds Nick seated across the desk from her boss, both men leaning toward each other and speaking quietly.

"Lauren, why don't you give us a minute," the mayor says.

She stiffens, unable to make sense of what's happening.

"Lauren?" The mayor again. "A minute, please. And close the door on your way out."

She backs away, shooting fire at Nick, who smiles benignly in return.

Planting herself by the closed door, she does her best to eavesdrop, but the door is solid oak and she doesn't capture much. She glances helplessly at the mayor's secretary, Dolores, a fixture in City Hall for a quarter of a century. The older woman stands and brings Lauren a drinking glass to place between her ear and the door. It helps, but only a little.

*   *   *

On the other side of the door: "As I was saying. I voted for you and intend to do so again, and it irks me that you're being set up to take the fall for the police department's failures."

"You and me both. Now, let's get back to the part about how I can fix it."

"Of course. Right now, and I say this with all due respect, you are the goat of the whole city. Pretty much every demographic group in Philadelphia County has lost faith in you."

Wallace Brown's eyes darken, and Nick can see he's not liking this part one bit. That's okay, though, because it shows how upset the man is.

"A big part of this is the Tick Tock killer, the idea that he's been running around shooting people for decades. Including that college kid, Dustin Ross."

"The commissioner tells me that's not the case. The police think he probably just got a hold of that damned gun."

"Mr. Smith. Yes. The police are almost certainly right about that. But the important thing is the public *thinks* he's been shooting people forever."

Nick pauses to let this sink in. Then, "It seems to me that getting this killer off the streets would be a huge step for you, as far as rehabilitating yourself in the public's eye."

Wallace Brown stares.

"I'd like to help you do that."

"And how, exactly, could you help? Are you telling me that you know the killer? Maybe he's a client of yours?"

Nick shakes his head. "Let's just say I know a guy who knows a guy."

"And you'd be willing to work your contacts, lead the police to the killer?"

"The police? You really want the cops to solve this problem? Get the credit? I don't see how that would help you one bit."

"Then, what're we talking here?"

"It's like I said, you're the goat right now. What you need is to become the hero."

"The hero." Wallace Brown repeats the word. "And this is something you can arrange?"

Nick leans forward, looks him in the eye. "That depends, Mr. Mayor. On how far you're prepared to think outside the box. And on how much personal courage you have," he adds, smiling to himself, knowing this is just the kind of bait a man like Wallace Brown would reach for.

* * *

Listening through the glass, Lauren can follow the cadence of the conversation, but not the details. Still, she picks up certain words and phrases, including, most alarmingly, repeated references to the Tick Tock killer, and to the mayor being a "hero."

"Jesus," she whispers. Nick knows the killer. And he's offering him up to the mayor. She feels nauseous.

* * *

Ten minutes later, Nick finishes his explanation and waits.

The mayor, sitting back in his chair, stares. After a while, he says, "I'd have to be crazy."

"It would be a bold move, that's for sure."

"I don't condone violence."

"Teddy Roosevelt. That's who I think would jump at this, in your position."

Wallace Brown tilts his head.

"Or Andrew Jackson. Old Hickory. Now there was a man willing to do what it took to get things done."

"I think we're done here." The mayor nods toward the door, telling Nick the meeting is over.

He thanks the mayor for his time, turns to go. He gets two steps before Wallace Brown calls out to him.

"You're here to take Lauren to lunch? You two are friends?"

Nick turns, sees the gleam in the mayor's eyes. "Friends, sure."

Wallace Brown smiles. "You're nailing that, aren't you?"

Nick shrugs.

The mayor chuckles. "Good man."

*   *   *

Lauren takes in the smug look on Nick's face when he opens the door, and it requires all her strength not to slap it off. Reaching behind him, she closes the door, hard, grabs his lapel and drags him into her own office.

"What the *hell,* Nick?"

"What?" All innocent.

"You come to *my* office, meet with *my* boss."

"You were in the ladies' room."

"Close the door on me."

"Guy talk."

"Fu—" She tries to drop the F-bomb, but she's so pissed, her throat closes before she can choke it out. She shoots him a furious look, reaches for her water bottle and takes a chug. Count to ten, she tells herself.

"I heard you through the door," she says. "You know who the killer is."

"That's crazy."

"He's a client of yours."

"No, he's not."

"You promised him to the mayor."

"No way."

"What's the angle here, Nick? What's in it for you?"

"I have no idea what you're talking about. Tick Tock came up in conversation, sure. Tell me someone who's not talking about him. But I don't know any more than anyone else."

"I can't believe you did this to me."

"I'll make it up at lunch. We'll go anywhere you want. And—"
he leans forward, smiling—"my friend's place at the Ritz is open
afterwards."

Her Smartwater bottle slams into the right side of Nick's face at
just under fourteen miles an hour. He's on his back, looking at the
ceiling, when she strides over, retrieves the bottle from the floor,
and empties it on his crotch.

"Aw, man," he says once his head clears and he realizes what she's
done.

By then, she's back at her desk, editing a press release.

She watches him struggle to get to his feet. When he opens his
mouth to say something, she puts up her hand. "Don't."

He lowers his head and leaves, grabbing a yellow legal pad from
the secretary's desk to cover his pants for the walk to his office.

CHAPTER FORTY-FOUR

RIZZO STARES NUMBLY at the polished wood coffin positioned atop the hole in the ground. Every now and then, he glances at the headstone, reads his father's name, birth and death dates, his description as the loving husband of Louise Rizzo.

"I don't think you ever told me her real name," says Sharon, standing next to him.

"Louise, until my father died. Then she switched to Eloise, which she thought sounded more glamorous. Then Elise, which sounded younger to her. Finally, Leeza, but she never explained why."

"She was one of a kind."

"That she was."

He pauses. "Thanks for doing this."

She takes his hand, leans in, kisses him on the cheek, neither one of them caring they're being watched by the small squadron of cops who showed up out of respect for Rizzo.

Along with the cops, he counts another dozen or so mourners. Marie from Sunset Senior Living, three or four of the residents, one in a wheelchair, the others who came with walkers, now sitting on wooden seats sinking in the soft ground. A couple of his mother's former neighbors are there, along with a woman she'd

grown up with who looks so old and frail Rizzo thinks she probably shouldn't bother leaving the cemetery.

They're all huddled under or just beyond the tent set up over
the grave. The weather-guessers predicted rain but were wrong
again. A fat yellow sun shines against a brilliant sky. Birds chirp.
Trees sway gently in a caressing breeze. The emerald grass is freshly
mowed, and dry.

A perfect day to not be dead, Rizzo thinks.

The priest is the big guy Leeza had a crush on, from Holy
Redeemer. Father Kane. The one with the crew cut and weathered
face. He catches the priest glancing his way, something in his eyes
besides sympathy for a decedent's son, and his cop hackles go up.

He stands stoically as the priest runs through the ashes-to-ashes
routine, after which the ceremony concludes with the placing of
roses on the coffin.

Sharon takes his arm and walks him back to the car. He senses
the other cops right behind them, surreptitiously trading glances,
shaking heads, but covering his back just the same. It's times like
this that make him glad he's a cop.

"Those three ladies who came from the home seemed pretty
upset," says Sharon once they're in the car.

He turns to her as she drives. "Mrs. Cranford and her cronies.
At war with Leeza from the day she moved in."

"Still, they were crying."

"They'll miss her. What else do old women have to do at a place
like that but nurse grudges and fight? Probably makes 'em feel
young, like they're back in high school."

"You have something set up at the old folks home?"

"A lunch," he says. "But I don't want to go there."

She nods. "I can fix you something at your place."

"That would be great."

They get to his house and he follows her to the kitchen. He sits at the table and she retrieves a beer from the refrigerator for him.

He watches her root through the fridge.

"You're not giving me a lot to work with here," she says.

"There's lobster mac and cheese."

She pulls out a plastic container, scoops out the white and yellowy goo, heats it in the microwave.

"I think this is part of your weight problem," she says, laying the plate on the table.

"You're the only one who seems to have a problem with my weight."

"Me and your heart."

"Lobster mac and cheese never killed anyone."

"I could probably name a hundred cardiologists who'd disagree."

"Yeah? Come up with ten and call it a win."

She shakes her head. "Just eat it."

He picks at the food; knows she's trying to read his thoughts. He wonders how close she's getting.

"Don't beat up on yourself, Ed."

Spot on.

"You did right by her."

"I'm not so sure," Rizzo says.

"She was in that place, what, three years? And you were there once, twice, three times a week. You took her out for dinner. Brought her here sometimes."

He nods.

"Not to mention handling all the drama. Smoothing out the messes she made."

"Notice her granddaughter wasn't there?"

"That's not on you."

"No?"

"You're thinking if you'd been a better father, Elizabeth would've been closer to her grandmother?"

"She wouldn't have fled to the West Coast to get away from me. That didn't do any good for her relationship with Leeza."

"You ever think the reason little Lizzy didn't show for her grandmother's funeral is because she's a self-centered shit?"

His eyes fill with fire.

"Sorry." She sits back, takes him in, this contradiction who let down his wife and daughter but then stepped up to the plate to care for his eccentric, high-maintenance mother.

"Is that what it was all about? Being there for Leeza to make up for being a lousy father, and husband?"

"I had people counting on me to take care of them, and I didn't. I made up my mind not to make the same mistake twice."

She reaches across the table, covers his hands with hers. "Well, you did it. You shouldered the burden. Carried your mother, the whole way to the finish line."

"Burden." He repeats the word. "It was a pain in the ass, sure. But it was good, too. She was always fun to watch. Even when I was a kid. And once she got into that place, and she got even crazier . . . sometimes I'd just sit back and listen to her rail on about this or that, and I'd be laughing my ass off, inside."

Sharon smiles, and they sit quietly for a while, until she takes his hands again.

"You know, Ed, it's okay to cry."

He looks at her, then looks away. His eyes glaze over, then start to well up. His lip quivers.

Later that night, lying in bed, still fully clothed, he turns to her.

"There was the other thing, too."

"What's that?"

"It gave me a purpose. Taking care of her." He looks at her, looking at him. "Who will I take care of now?"

CHAPTER FORTY-FIVE

LAUREN DEVEREUX STANDS on the corner of 18th and Walnut waiting for the light to turn so she can cross the street for a pleasant lunch in Rittenhouse Square. She'll find an open bench, put on her earbuds, eat her salad, and zone out for an hour or so.

It's been three days since that shit Nick Loughead humiliated her in her own office. He'd been calling her since, trying to patch things up, but she was done with him. He'd been nothing more to her than a crutch—someone to spend time with while she focused on her political career. But it was time she started looking around for someone to have a serious relationship with, maybe even marry.

She was done with the mayor, too. In teaming up with Wallace Brown, she'd picked the wrong horse to ride; that was obvious to her now. Even if he survived his present ordeal, it was clear to her that he lacked the mettle to rise to national office. But her dream had always been to land in Washington, so it was time to leverage her contacts, find a link to someone already working there, a lobbyist or congressman, hopefully someone single, and jump ship.

But that can wait an hour.

She takes a deep breath, pushes her problems from her mind, and focuses on the beautiful day and the lovely lunch she's about to have.

It's then that she notices the truck. It's black and big and old and dirty. Very dirty. A heavy-duty Mack Tri-Axel dump truck. A black canvas tarp is stretched across its giant bed. It doesn't look like it belongs on Walnut Street near Rittenhouse Square. Still, it lumbers along in the traffic, approaching the intersection.

The light turns green in Lauren's favor, but she doesn't move, just stares at the truck, now sitting first in line at the red. The windshield is smeared, but she can make out the driver. Something about him looks familiar.

The light changes and the truck inches its way into the intersection. It stops halfway through, then reverses course and turns so that its rear end backs over the sidewalk and toward the northeast entrance of the park.

Horns blare. People curse. Then the tide turns, from anger to concern. Something bad is about to happen, in this post-9/11 world.

People on the sidewalk abutting the park scamper away from the truck. Cars rush through the intersection, their drivers trying to place distance between themselves and the truck before the inevitable explosion.

And then it happens. With the truck's tail end now almost up to the concrete pillars framing the entrance to the park, its thick hydraulic arm pushes the truck-bed into the air. Higher and higher it goes.

Lauren stands frozen in place fifty feet away, unable to tear her eyes from the spectacle, unable to lift her feet from the pavement.

For a moment, the whole world is in suspended animation. Everyone stands staring at the truck. Waiting.

Then the truck's cargo begins sliding onto the pavement behind it.

And the people scream.

It's bodies. Five, ten, a dozen, two dozen, more, the pile growing first in height then length as the truck pulls forward to make room.

"It's dead people!"

"My God!"

"Oh God!"

"Oh my God!"

"They robbed them from graves," someone shouts.

Gaping at the bodies, Lauren agrees the corpses certainly look like they've been pulled from the soil. Their clothes are filthy, and in tatters. Their faces are bluish and sunken. The open mouths on some of them reveal teeth blackened, or missing. Open eyes are unfocused.

The bodies stop dropping and the truck's driver lowers the bed. He turns west on Walnut Street and drives away. But not before glancing at Lauren.

It's then Lauren realizes who he is. It's the man from the Rivera Recreation Center. The one who stood and told the mayor he and his group were going to take matters into their own hands if something wasn't done about El Campamento.

Her eyes wide, Lauren turns from the driver back to the pile of bodies. From somewhere inside it, she senses movement. The other horrified onlookers do, too, and someone shouts, "It's moving!" People with their hands over their mouths. People with hands cupping the sides of their heads.

Then, it makes its appearance and someone shouts, "WTF!"

"What is that thing?"

Blazing white teeth in a black snout, pushing through the top of the pile. And something in the teeth.

"My God, it's a finger!"

More screaming. More gasping.

It's just a dog, Lauren realizes, watching the star-chested pittie extricate itself, descend the pile, then run across the park, the index finger protruding from its mouth like a flesh-colored cigar. Still she remains frozen, now with terror. Because she knows what's coming. She knows what the pile really is. Bodies, for sure. And yet not.

It only takes a minute or so for her fears to be confirmed.

"It's moving!"

"The pile is moving!"

And it does. All at once, it seems, the bodies begin to writhe, and wiggle. Arms outstretch. Feet kick. Eyes open. Groans escape from mouths.

And then they stand and start walking.

Muffled screams wrap themselves around Lauren's dazed consciousness.

More screams. And then the word Lauren knows is coming.

"Zombies!"

"They're fucking zombies!"

The onlookers scatter, desperate to flee the flesh-craving corpses they've all seen in the movies, and on TV.

But these are a different species of zombie, Lauren knows, and it's not flesh they crave, but opioids. "Heroin zombies," she says. Heroin zombies brought fresh from El Campamento. Loaded, undoubtedly, onto the truck by a small army of angry Kensingtonians, driven by one of their leaders to the heart of Center City.

Lauren's cellphone rings in her pocket and she knows who it is without looking. She knows, too, that a hundred other calls are being placed at this very minute, and soon it will be a thousand, to every major news outlet in the country.

As if on cue, a Channel 3 news van screeches to a halt on Walnut Street, the cameraman and reporter scrambling to get into position. Police cars arrive en masse, and more local news vans. Around the country, she knows, flights and hotels are being booked. Anderson will be here within hours, maybe even Wolf himself.

Philadelphia will become ground zero of the opioid crisis, the heroin zombies the half-living feast from which a million delicious sound bites will be chewed on the TV news shows.

Lauren's phone is still ringing, and she pulls it out and answers.

"*Where the hell are you?*" Wallace Brown.

"At the zombie apocalypse."

CHAPTER FORTY-SIX

"This is a goddamned disaster."

Wallace Brown pacing around his office, pulling out his hair. Lauren watching him, wondering where to begin her search for a new job.

"You know who's going to get blamed for this, don't you? Me! That's who."

Duh.

"And you know why?"

The voice inside Lauren's head says, *Because you're the mayor. Because you could have pressured Conrail to clean up El Campamento. Because you could have ordered the police to drag the addicts from the tracks and put them into rehab.*

"Because people are always looking for a scapegoat. Doesn't matter these problems are intractable. That the experts can't agree on how to fix them. That they've been passed down from one administration to the next."

"Let me pour you a drink, sir," Lauren says.

"Kicking the can, that's all this is. Has nothing to do with me. Sooner or later the music was going to stop, and whoever was sitting in my chair was going to be left holding the bag."

She tilts her head, wondering at Wallace Brown's penchant for jumbling metaphors. "Macallan or Glenlivet?"

Her boss unable to make a decision, she pours from both bottles, hands him the glass. He takes a hefty sip. Then another.

"I need time to think," he says, flopping into his chair. "Which was this, the Macallan or the Glenlivet?"

"Yes."

"Well, bring me the bottle. Then shut the door on your way out."

She brings him a bottle of Belvenie 14 year, a gift from some businessman or politician seeking to curry favor, then hurriedly leaves him to his thoughts.

*　　*　　*

Three blocks away on North 15th Street, the phone on Nick Loughead's desk begins to ring. His head pounding, he covers his ears, closes his eyes, and curses the girl at Delilah's for grossly overserving him the night before. Curses himself for blowing so much money. How many twenties had he stuffed down panties and G-strings? Too many to count. But not enough to deaden the dread gnawing at his brain because of the impending loss of his building thanks to that schmuck from L&I.

The ringing stops for a minute. Then cruelly starts up again.

"What? *What?*"

A pause at the other end. Then, "Mr. Loughead? This is the mayor."

He bolts up in his seat.

"Have you been watching the news?"

"I'm preparing for trial. No time for anything else."

"Well, some things have been happening, and I'm willing to reconsider your offer. About the Tick Tock killer."

"I see." He rushes to the TV, turns it on, thinking something big must've happened. With every station covering the zombie attack on Rittenhouse Square, it takes about two seconds to see that it has.

"Just how certain are you that you can make this work?"

He smiles. "How certain are you, Mr. Mayor, that you have the right stuff to pull it off?" Turn the tables, make it about the other man's fortitude. Make it a personal challenge.

"I'm not worried about me. I'm the half of this equation I have no doubts about. What I'm asking is—are you sure you can set this up *right*? So that it goes down the way it needs to."

Before Nick has time to answer, the mayor says, "This phone isn't tapped, is it? You don't record calls coming into your office."

"Wouldn't be very smart of a criminal defense attorney to tape his phone conversations, Mr. Mayor."

Wallace chuckles. "No, I don't suppose it would."

"As for your question, don't worry. I'll set this up in a way that's foolproof. You'll have all the advantages. He'll be taken completely by surprise."

"About the timing—"

"ASAP. That's what I'd recommend, based upon what I'm seeing on the TV. And in that regard, the timing of this zombie thing might work out perfectly for you."

"How d'you figure?"

"The star reporters from every network in the country will be here to sing your praises for ridding the city of a maniacal killer."

"And the police won't get any credit?"

"Not a bit. It'll be all you. Wallace Brown. Hero-mayor of Philadelphia."

He envisions the mayor nodding his head.

"Think about it. How many mayors of major American cities have faced off against mass-murdering serial killers and lived to tell the tale?"

"Uh . . ."

"Zero. That's how many."

No response.

"Of course . . ." He lets the words hang in the air.

"Of course what?" Wallace Brown blurts out.

He knows what's coming, Nick thinks. So he explains his mold problem with L&I, tells the mayor what needs to be done. Not as a supplicant, but as a peer, one businessman entering into an agreement with another, each knowing that both have to get what they want or neither will walk away with a deal. He keeps his voice steady, confident. *These are my terms.*

As he expects, the mayor agrees without protest, without petty haggling, saying, "Don't worry about L&I. I'll get them off your back right quick. I think this whole mold thing is overblown, anyway."

"Great. Now let's put our heads together."

*   *   *

Nick hangs up the phone, tickled he'd been able so quickly to hammer out a solid plan for how the mayor would confront and kill Tick Tock. He'd always prided himself on his skills as a legal tactician. He's delighted to find his genius transfers to physical combat as well. He'd have made a great general.

The next step is to lay it out for his nincompoop uncle. He's waiting now for the old man to answer the phone.

"My favorite nephew."

The singsong southern drawl makes Nick cringe.

"It's all set, on this end," Nick says.

"What is?"

"The plan to get rid of your killer."

Deke pauses. "Give it to me. I'll be the judge whether it's set or not."

Nick pushes down his anger and lays it out.

He's met with silence.

"Well?"

"You're telling me you ran this by the mayor and he's up for it?"

"On board a hundred percent. You been watching the news, about the heroin zombies? He's desperate. Tick Tock will refocus the media, turn him into a hero."

"How's your hero with a gun?"

"Says he's pretty good. Belongs to a gun club. Shoots pistol, rifle. Shotgun, too. He says he's won some awards."

"He ever been in combat? Fired a weapon while looking down the barrel of a gun pointed back at him?"

"Does that matter?"

"Christ, boy."

"He'll be ready. Just run it by your guy."

"I don't know. I can't see him going for it. He's smart enough to know that killing the mayor would make him the focus of an all-out manhunt. He'd find himself in the crosshairs of the police, the DA, and the FBI."

"Just make the offer."

"What is the offer?"

"Tell him the job will pay $250,000. Fifty up front, the rest the day after the job's done."

"That politician has a quarter mil?"

Nick fights to keep the exasperation out of his voice. "Uncle, he doesn't need it. Your guy will be dead, remember? And we can split the $50K advance, if you can find it afterward." He knows his uncle will never own up to finding the money, but he doesn't care. He'll rake in a lot more when he sells his building, which shouldn't be a problem when the L&I investigation is wiped from the books.

"I'll run it by him. But I'm not making any promises. You better come up with another plan."

They hang up and Nick exhales.

"Thank God," he says. "Praise Jesus." Maybe someone up there is looking out for him after all.

CHAPTER FORTY-SEVEN

REMI SITTING ACROSS the desk from Deke, the door closed. The small room filled with smoke. Deke's cigar burnt down to a nub.

"Look, I know it sounds crazy," Deke says, something in Remi's eyes worrying him, making him think he's pushed the man too far with the idea of killing the mayor.

Remi stares, watches his boss shift in his seat.

"I'm in."

"Huh? I mean, that's great." But to Deke, it seems to have been too easy a sell. He stares at Remi. "There's something personal going on here. You know him."

"I know him." Remi stands. "Get it arranged. The sooner the better."

*　*　*

Deke watches Remi leave the office, walk down the center aisle, leave the building. He lifts the receiver on his phone, to dial his nephew, share the good news that they'll both be rid of the loose cannon. "The sooner the better," he says.

CHAPTER FORTY-EIGHT

THE DAY AFTER the zombie apocalypse and Remi and Kayla are at the Empire Diner eating dinner. Her finishing off her hamburger, slurping the last of her chocolate shake. Him picking at a turkey club.

Something's eating at him, she can see it on his face. "Not hungry?"

"Had a big lunch at the garage."

"Baloney and cheese sandwich, some chips?" She'd packed it herself. "That's what you call a big lunch?"

She watches him start to formulate a fib, but he gives up, just shrugs.

"You're looking old, Remi."

He chuckles, but she hears bitterness in the laugh.

"You ready to tell me what's going on yet?"

Again, he starts and stops. After a minute, he half-heartedly offers, "You need to keep your mind on your schoolwork."

"Why? I'm already accepted at Penn. My guidance counselor says it's okay if I get a B."

"There'll be no Bs in that bonnet," he says, nodding to the top of her head.

"No slowing before the finish line," she says, one of the lines he'd repeated to her a million times as she grew up.

She studies him and her smile fades. He's never been one to hunch over the table, let his shoulders sink. But he's so stooped it almost seems like he's melting.

"Oh! I almost forgot to tell you. The mayor's assistant called. The mayor's inviting me and Sandra back to his office. Of all the kids from the leadership thing, he thinks Sandra and I had the most potential. Isn't that grea . . . What? *What?*"

She leans back, struck by the steel in his eyes, his suddenly rigid posture.

"Jeez. You'd think I was pointing a gun at you. It's an honor. Not an insult."

He exhales, relaxes, with effort, she can tell.

"I'll think about it."

She locks eyes with him. *Why don't you trust me? Just tell me, whatever it is, and we can work through it.*

He reaches across the table, pats her face, winks. It's all forced, she knows, but at least he knows it's hurting her that he isn't opening up. That'll have to be enough for now.

*   *   *

He glances at her on the drive home. She has her earbuds in and is rocking to the music that he, thankfully, can't hear.

He tries to focus on his driving, but his attention keeps getting drawn to his heart. His right hand on the wheel, he surreptitiously presses his chest with the long fingers of his left hand, pretending he's just scratching.

Last night he had a scare. A bad one. Kayla had long gone to bed. He was in the bathroom, brushing his teeth. He leaned down to rinse, and the next thing he knew, he woke up on the floor, drenched in sweat, and urine. His heart must've given out. Practice for the big event, coming any time now, he figured. It shook him up, kept him awake half the night, fighting sleep.

He's going to leave Kayla, nothing he can do about that. But he can't let himself be taken before he tick tocks Wallace Brown. No way he's gonna let that bastard swoop in after he's gone and mess Kayla up like he did her mother.

He glances at her again, his heart breaking. He'd seen the pain in her eyes from him not being honest about what is happening. They never kept secrets from each other. It was one of the reasons their relationship was so strong. That, and their loss of Beatrice.

"Hey," he says.

She looks at him, pulls out her earbuds.

"Soon," he says. "Soon."

And he sees she knows what he means.

CHAPTER FORTY-NINE

TWO DAYS AFTER his mother's funeral and the infamous zombie invasion, Rizzo and Flynn buckle their seat belts.

"Where to?" asks Flynn.

"Gladwyne. Going to shake the Maleena tree. See if any fruit falls off."

Flynn starts the car and off they go.

Rizzo in the passenger seat, staring ahead, not feeling like talking, senses Flynn glance at him from time to time.

"I'm fine," he says, annoyed.

"A tough thing, when you lose a parent. I know—my old man died the summer after I graduated high school. Forty-five years old, the picture of health, and he dropped dead grilling chicken in our backyard."

Rizzo looks out the side window, doing his best to ignore his partner.

"Massive heart attack. That's what the doctor said."

"Why do people insist on—"

"My mother never got over it."

"I swear, I'm going to shoot myself, you keep on with this."

"I was just trying—"

"Well, stop. It doesn't do any good."

They drive the rest of the way in silence. Flynn pulls into the long driveway and parks in the circle by the front door.

"Remember what I told her about the handcuffs? About finding her husband's killer and cuffing them and taking them away?"

"Yeah," Flynn says.

"Well, watch."

Rizzo pauses at the threshold but doesn't ring the bell. Instead, he opens the unlocked door and leads Flynn into the giant marble-floored foyer. They stand there, waiting.

After a few moments, Maleena makes her appearance at the top of the stairs. Absorbed in her nails, she doesn't notice them until she's halfway down. "What the . . ."

She pauses.

Rizzo reaches around his back, pulls out the handcuffs and lets them dangle.

Maleena's eyes grow wide with terror. Then, after a minute they flare. "That effing Nick! That bastard."

Rizzo calmly walks toward the stairs, swinging the cuffs.

"He ratted me out. I knew better than to trust him."

"You should've come to us first, Mrs. Roseman. Then the deal would've been yours, not his."

"That son-of-a-bitch."

Rizzo waves her to come down. "Come on, let's get you to central booking."

"He's as bad as Hal. All the times I had to screw that fat old bastard and he left me with nothing. And now, thanks to Nick, I'm going to go to jail."

"It's not going to be that bad," Rizzo says. "Ever see that show *Orange Is the New Black*?"

She begins to sway, puts her hand on the banister to steady herself.

"You need me to help you?"

She says no and starts down, but then stops. "I have to pee. Is there time for me to pee?"

Rizzo looks to Flynn and they both shrug. "Sure, but don't take too long. We got to get you to the station. Do the Miranda thing, take your statement."

Her shoulders slump and she slowly ascends the stairs, turns down a hallway. Rizzo and Flynn hear her close the bathroom door.

They wait for a while, walk around the foyer, comment on the artwork, how big the place is. Wait some more, looking at their watches. Then, with a start, Rizzo says, "Shit."

Rizzo races up the stairs, pushes open the bathroom door, and there she is, as he feared, on the floor. Rizzo sees the empty pill bottle in the sink, tells Flynn to dial 911 as they lift Maleena to her feet.

"Come on, sweetheart," Rizzo says. "You have to walk around. Stay awake."

She bobbles her head in his direction, her eyes out of focus.

"Try to talk. Tell me more about this shit Nick who ratted you out. How much you hate him." Hoping she'll say his last name.

Rizzo and Flynn manage to get Maleena downstairs in time for the ambulance. She rambles the whole time, but her speech is incoherent.

In the car on the way to the hospital, Rizzo says, "So now we're looking for a guy named Nick. How many Nicks do you think live in Philadelphia?"

"You ever do that routine before?" asks Flynn. "With the cuffs?"

"A hundred times."

"How often does it work?"

"This is the first time."

* * *

Rizzo and Flynn on the way to the hospital, neither saying anything, until Flynn asks, "Did it upset you? When she said that thing about her husband being fat?"

"Upset me? Why would that upset me?"

Flynn doesn't answer, so he looks over at him, catches Flynn smiling.

"You're a prick. You know that, Flynn?" Thinking: *I'm liking this kid more every day.*

CHAPTER FIFTY

LAUREN DEVEREUX IS WORRIED. The phones are ringing off the hook, reporters from around the country pressing to interview the mayor about the zombie attack two days ago, about the raging opioid epidemic his administration has failed to address, about El Campamento, about the city's record-setting number of unsolved murders, about his catastrophic failure as mayor of the nation's sixth largest city. Meanwhile, City Hall itself is surrounded by news vans, protesters, and mounted and unmounted police officers.

What's worrying Lauren, though, isn't any of that, but her normally stressed-out boss' reaction to it. Wallace Brown is prancing around his office seemingly lighter than air. A man without a care in the world.

For the second day in a row this has been going on. The mayor's secretary, Dolores, told Lauren she thinks Wallace is having a nervous breakdown. When the mayor returned from lunch carrying flowers for the office, Lauren had to fight Dolores to keep her from calling an ambulance. "The man isn't right in the head," Dolores had told her. "I think he's over-medicating."

Through her doorway, Lauren glances at the secretary, who looks back and shakes her head.

The phone rings and Lauren watches Dolores pick it up.

"Uh-huh," she says. "Uh-huh." Then, looking at Lauren, she rings through to the mayor, telling him, "Mr. Nick Loughead is on the line. Yes, I'll close your door."

Lauren stands and walks to the mayor's door just as Dolores closes it, a routine they've practiced each of the three times Nick has called over the past two days. Also part of the routine: Dolores handing the glass to Lauren so she can eavesdrop through the door.

Most of what the mayor says is indiscernible. Still, she's been getting better at picking out key words and phrases the mayor seems to repeat in each of the conversations, including *tick tock* and *news*, *hero*, and *ha!* Most curiously, she's picked up *mold* and *L&I*, though she can't fathom what either would have to do with the Tick Tock killer.

One more word, new to today's conversation, raises the hairs on Lauren's neck. The word is *tonight*.

The mayor hangs up and Lauren stands, pulls the glass from her ear, and walks back into her office.

"Oh shit."

Something's going to happen with the killer, tonight. But if that's the case, why isn't the mayor talking to the police about it? Maybe the police already know. Maybe her boss is secretly working hand in hand with the cops to bring in the killer. She considers the possibility but dismisses it; there are few secrets in City Hall and none in the mayor's office. At least nothing that's secret from her.

No, whatever Wallace Brown's doing, he's doing on his own. Him and Nick, that scheming, self-enamored pustule.

She picks up her cell, dials Loughead's burner phone, and is sent directly to voicemail. "Unbelievable."

Hanging up the phone, she walks into the foyer in time to catch her boss telling Dolores he's going to be working late. "Would you mind calling that Chinese place on Seventh and Market, have them bring me some kung pao chicken with white rice? And some pork dumplings."

"You need me to work late, boss?" Lauren asks.

"Oh, no, no. No need for that."

Lauren's stomach drops. He's never said no before to the idea of her staying late with him. And she's wearing a short skirt today, with a sleeveless shirt. Something is very wrong.

CHAPTER FIFTY-ONE

NINE O'CLOCK. Rizzo and Sharon sitting on the couch, streaming *Yellowstone*.

"I still can't believe it worked," he says.

"Is this real leather? How old is this thing?"

"All the times I've done the handcuff thing and no one ever fell for it. Except her."

"Hundredth time's the charm. How's she doing?"

"I called the hospital just before you came over. The doctors say she'll be fine."

"I don't think you had enough to arrest her."

"I wasn't arresting her. That would've come later, at the station, once she confessed everything in detail, and gave me her accomplice's last name. That's when I would've Mirandized her."

"She thought you were arresting her."

"She might have been confused on that issue."

"And you went in without knocking."

"The door was wide open."

"Flynn will back you up on that?"

"He's my partner."

"You know that when she wakes up tomorrow with a clear head, she's going to lawyer up."

"Pisses me off the doctors wouldn't let me talk to her in the hospital. All I needed was a last name."

"You'll have to let her go."

He sighs. "You're probably right."

"You go through her mail?"

"Soon as the ambulance left. Nothing from an insurance company. Lots of envelopes, from Neiman Marcus, Nordstrom's, Bloomingdale's."

"So we still have no leads on Tick Tock."

"We need to find out who Nick is."

"English name for the devil. Old Nick."

*   *   *

Deke and Remi sitting across Deke's desk.

"I just don't know how you can be so sure he'll be working this late," Remi says.

"I told you, we got someone on the inside. He told my guy the mayor's been holed up in his office for two days. Afraid to leave because the protesters and reporters hound him like dogs. He's there now, and he'll be there when you show up."

"Alone."

"City Hall, after five p.m.? Of course, he'll be alone."

"Uh-huh. And all these doors will be unlocked?" Remi points at a diagram of City Hall, red circles around the doors he's to use.

"The outside door will be. For the inside doors, you use that," pointing to an attorney access card. "My guy got it from a maintenance guy who works at City Hall. He found it on the floor." Deke chuckles. "Some poor schmuck lawyer's going to get the surprise of his life when the police IT guys see it was his card. Guy's going to wake up to find his house surrounded by SWAT cops."

"I don't like the idea that some other guy is going to take the rap for this."

"Oh, relax. He'll be cleared by morning. Then he'll probably hire another lawyer to sue the city for false arrest and defamation. Guy'll take home a million bucks."

"This is the last time."

"I heard you. I get it."

Remi stands, looks at his watch. "I'll work for another hour, then head into the city."

*　　*　　*

Deke watches him leave the office, walk to a car he's working on. Watches him lean into the open hood, study what's inside.

It'll be a shame to lose a guy like that, man who knows cars like he does. A quiet guy, too, not one to stir up trouble. A man who keeps his nose to the grindstone, does his job, and doesn't whine about hard work. But the killing thing has changed him, brought out something dark inside, a creature with a steady killing hand and a heart so cold he can torment his victims with the tick tock thing before he fires.

He leans over, pulls out his bottle, and pours. The phone rings as he lifts his glass, the caller ID telling him it's his wife. He tosses back the glass, lets the call go to voicemail. He knows she's calling for him to come home and help her with their weepy daughter and her two screaming kids, the three of them tossed onto the street with her no-account husband because he hadn't paid the landlord for half a year.

No way he's taking her calls, and no way he's leaving here until he gets the word that Remi Bone is dead.

CHAPTER FIFTY-TWO

Nick Loughead sitting in his office three blocks from City Hall, his Glock on the desk in front of him.

He hears a bump and reaches for the gun, stands up. He points the pistol toward his open office door. He's done the same thing three or four times now, jumping at every noise, thinking it might be the killer coming to whack him before he does the mayor.

He listens and watches and waits, does his best to laser-focus his senses. But nothing happens and, after a long time, he exhales and sits.

He glances at the phone, expecting another ring from Lauren any minute now, her calls coming in all day, the messages angrier and angrier. He thinks about the time they were both still students and he nailed her in their law school library, and the memory makes him smile. He's going to miss her. But Maleena's just as hot and with the money she'll be coming into, he's hoping he can persuade her to pay for some trips to the islands. She's still mad at him because the killer botched her husband's murder the first time, but once the dough rolls in, she'll forgive him—he's sure of it.

He stands and paces. He doesn't like that his whole future depends on another person, especially someone like Wallace Brown. He'd done his best to idiot-proof his plan, make sure the mayor doesn't screw it up and get himself killed. But the mayor's increasing overconfidence as the thing approaches is worrisome. It's like he doesn't get that there will be *two* men with guns at the OK Corral. Part of that is Nick's own fault, the mayor having initially been so nervous that Nick suggested he wear a Kevlar vest.

"The killer always shoots through the heart," he'd said. "With the vest, even if he gets off a shot after you do, you'll be okay."

So yesterday, Wallace had pressured one of the officers on his security force to dig up an extra vest for him. Since then, he'd been talking like he was Iron Man, phrases like "bring him on," and "let's get this done," and "time's up, motherfuck," rolling off his tongue.

To take his mind off things, Nick sits in front of his computer, brings up Zillow. There are some nice office buildings for sale in Center City, places built to be private mansions but later renovated for commercial use. He should easily be able to afford one once he sells his current building, which is worth three million, or will be once the mayor makes the mold thing go way. He's still amazed how easily the building fell into his lap three years ago; one of his clients, a big-time dealer, set him up as a straw man to buy the place in his own name, giving him the cash to acquire it outright, and telling him no one in the dealer's organization or family knew about the purchase. Two weeks later, the client was blown up in his car and the building was his.

"Everything works out like it should," he says. What his mother told him when he was a kid, always worried about something or other. He looks up at the ceiling, says, "I hope you're with me now, Mom."

He makes the sign of the cross.

* * *

The Honorable Wallace Brown looking down at his watch to check the time. Eleven p.m. He'd just gotten the call from Nick Loughead, who'd just gotten the call from the killer's boss. Tick Tock is on his way. Should be there in about forty-five minutes.

He takes a deep breath, checks his desk to make sure everything's in order. Directly in front of him on the blotter is an old-fashioned brass bookstand, the kind you use to prop a book on, and he has—the Bible. He'll hold the gun right behind the book, using it to block Tick Tick's line of sight to the gun. The instant the killer walks in, he'll lift the gun and shoot. The killer, thinking he has time to give his tick tock speech, won't be ready to fire.

After it's done, Wallace has decided that he'll stand over the killer's body and say the words. "Tick tock says the clock. Time's up, motherfuck." Wallace smiles, liking the way the words roll off his tongue.

Not every man is given the chance to prove his mettle, he knows, see how he holds up in physical peril. In some ways, he's glad it's come to this. How's that saying go? It's not what happens to you, it's how you deal with it that defines you. Well, he's about to show the world. All those parasites in the press, the community activists with too much time on their hands, the incompetent police, the cable news pundits saying his political career is swirling around the toilet bowl. They'd swarmed on him like a plague of locusts attacking a wheat field. They think he's history. But he's about to make history! He'll be the only big-city mayor ever to go toe-to-toe with a mass murderer and live to tell about it.

He moves the book an inch or so to the left, adjusts the gun a little. He pats the thick Kevlar vest underneath his white shirt.

He leans back in his chair and lets his thoughts drift. After a minute, they land on Kayla Washington, and her mother, Beatrice.

Now there was a troublesome woman, one who constantly needed to be put in line, not like his wife, Phyllis, respectful like a woman should be. And quiet, most of the time, though even she does need to be shown her place every now and then.

He can still remember the day Beatrice told him she was pregnant. How angry he was, her supposedly on birth control, but obviously lying about it. He'd known from the outset that she wasn't one to marry, and the kid sure wasn't going to change that. So he shook the dust off his feet and never looked back, the woman and her child being books that needed to be closed and put on the shelf.

He never gave them a moment's thought, until that nutjob—some guy she was seeing—showed up and sucker punched him. But he got the last laugh on that numbnut, sending two detectives to beat the shit out of him. He was an assistant district attorney at the time, still on the same team as the cops who were always ready to lay out some lowlife who crossed the line.

And now here comes the child, young Kayla, a student leader, a scholar telling him she's going off to Penn. A beautiful girl obviously in awe of him, respectful of his position and open to his guidance. So why not, after all this time, and with her mother dead, give that guidance? Why not come into the girl's life? Shape her. Show her the way the world works.

Who was going to get in the way? Some greasy-handed mechanic?

He chuckles at the idea.

CHAPTER FIFTY-THREE

LAUREN TOSSES AND TURNS. She can't get to sleep. The thing with the mayor and Nick and Tick Tock has her head spinning. Something's going to go down and it's going to happen tonight.

She gets up, walks to the living room, turns on the news to see if Tick Tock has been captured or killed. The lead story, as is the case with all lead stories in the past two days, is about the heroin zombies taking over Rittenhouse Square. The angle Anchorman Jim is working tonight is about how hard it's been for the police to round up and lasso all the zombies because of the number of alleys and dumpsters around the square.

Jimbo does mention Tick Tock, but only to warn viewers that he's still out there and that the police have no leads.

"Shit."

She has to warn somebody about her concerns, but who?

* * *

Sharon reaches over Rizzo to the bed-stand for her cellphone. She looks at the number. It isn't familiar, but something tells her to take the call, rather than screen it via voicemail.

She listens as Lauren identifies herself and explains why she's calling.

"You're saying you think the mayor and this guy you've been seeing know something about the Tick Tock killer? And something's going to happen with the killer tonight?" She says the words out loud as she pokes Rizzo in the ribs, to get him to wake up and pay attention. He sits up in bed and she holds out the phone so he can hear.

"Yes. And the mayor's working late tonight. Very late, as in I'm pretty sure he's still there."

"And that's unusual?"

"Wallace Brown working after eleven p.m.? Oh, yeah."

"Your boyfriend. What's his name?"

"He's not my boyfriend. He's a slime-oozing slug in human form."

"And his name is?"

"Nick. Nick Loughead." She glances at Rizzo, who jumps from the bed and starts to put his clothes on.

"What's his address?"

"I don't know his home address. But his office is on 15th Street, a couple blocks north of City Hall. There's a big sign for Kiddie Karate on the first floor. His office is on the second."

"Kiddie Karate building?" She repeats it for Rizzo, who gets the message and nods.

"Is there anything else you can tell us?"

"Us?"

Sharon doesn't explain.

"Well, maybe one thing. The mayor's been acting weird. He's in deep shit because of the zombie thing and the opioid epidemic. And all the unsolved murders—"

"Well, if the public would help us out a little—"

"But he's been dancing around the office like he's just won a popularity contest."

"So he knows something."

"That's what I've been telling you."

"You did the right thing by calling me. I'll get ahold of the detective leading the Tick Tock investigation."

"Will you be able to reach him, this late?"

"I already have."

Lauren pauses. "Oh. I see." And she does.

"You, me, and the wall, okay?"

"I get it."

Lauren hangs up.

"I know that building," Rizzo says. "The Kiddie Karate place."

"You're going there now?"

"First, I'll pay a visit to the mayor."

"Who should I call for backup?"

He stares at her. "Let's not jump the gun."

"She thinks something's going down, like now."

"Maybe. But whatever it is, it won't happen in the mayor's office."

"Your cop intuition?"

"Hasn't failed me yet."

"Then why go?"

"Because if she's right, the mayor knows where it *is* going down."

"And he'll just tell you?"

"We have a history. He owes me."

"Uh-huh."

"And if he doesn't want to help, I'll toss out a few enticements. Break the ice with helpful phrases like 'obstruction of justice.'"

"You know he was a DA, right?"

Rizzo leans in, kisses her on the cheek.

"Call me," she says. "Let me know what happens."

He winks, and leaves.

CHAPTER FIFTY-FOUR

REMI BONE, in his truck now, on the way to do the deed one last time. And this time not only for money to send Kayla to school, but to protect her from an animal.

After Beatrice finally broke down and told him all the terrible things Wallace Brown had done to her, it made his blood boil so badly he felt like he was on fire. It was all he could do to stop at hitting the man and putting him down. Standing over Wallace Brown, what he wanted more than anything was to kneel on his chest and pummel his face until it wasn't a face.

But he'd have done Bea and Kayla no good rotting in prison. So he walked away, thinking that would be the end of it. Thinking the big man would be too embarrassed to tell anyone what happened. Not thinking the man would send two cop goons to beat him to a pulp.

He was angry at Wallace Brown, but more angry at himself for making such a stupid move, and for not seeing what such a man might do to get even, embarrassed or not. But he'd swallowed his anger, nursed his wounds, and moved on.

It was the right thing to do. And what he was going to do tonight was the right thing, too. The things the mayor said to

Kayla made clear the man was planning to move in, and once Remi was dead, there'd be no one to stop him.

A man who does terrible things to his woman will do terrible things to his child. All you had to do was pick up a paper or watch the news to know that. Kayla, as strong and smart as she is, would end up meat in Wallace Brown's grinder.

He can't just tell her about the mayor. That would be cruel: *Hey, sweetheart, your mom left her man because he abused her emotionally, and beat her, beat her bad. And that powerful politician you admire so much, the great leader who told you how special you are, that's the man.*

"No, sir, I could never tell her that. She can't find out that monster is her biological father."

That's what he said to Butch Kane that afternoon, when he went to see him one last time. The priest sat back in his chair and took it all in, then repeated what he'd told Remi before, that killing is wrong and that's all there is to it.

When he stopped talking, they sat and stared at each other until Remi asked if the father would mind giving him the wafer. Old Butch—and that's who he was looking like at that point—left the room for a minute and came back with the gold goblet.

"Repeat after me, Remi," he'd said. "Lord, I am not worthy you should enter under my roof, but only say the word and my soul shall be healed."

Remi said the words and Butch gave him the Eucharist. Then, Butch said the words, too, and ate some magic bread himself.

Afterward, the priest led him to the church and they prayed a while in the first pew. Then, when they were still on their knees, the priest looked over at him.

"Remi, please don't do this."

He looked down.

"Please, Remi."

He got all choked up, tried to explain he had no choice. But all that came out was a single word: "Kayla."

Butch Kane looked at him with the saddest eyes he'd ever seen. Then, he turned away, and prayed quietly. After a while, Remi stood up and left, patting the priest on his shoulder.

CHAPTER FIFTY-FIVE

HE PARKS THE truck in the Love Park underground garage. It's late so he has to leave by walking up the ramp. Once he's outside, he walks down 15th Street to JFK, crosses to Dilworth Plaza. One of the outside tower doors is unlocked, as he was told it would be. The inside doors respond to his access card. He walks up the steps to the second floor, walks down a hall to the mayor's suite.

He enters quietly. He'll take the man by surprise. Say the words, pull the trigger. One through the heart.

He walks through the foyer to the mayor's office. The door is open. He enters, expecting to see the mayor busy at work, head down, studying his papers. But the man is looking right at him.

* * *

Wallace Brown hears the footsteps. The killer is trying to be quiet, and he probably wouldn't have heard the man if he weren't expecting him.

He's ready, looking forward to it, in fact. Looking forward to seeing the smug look on Old Tick Tock's face change to terror when he sees the gun pointing back at him before the killer even has a chance to raise up Mr. Smith and say his words.

But the man enters and everything changes as soon as he sees his face. It's older now, though no heavier. His hair is grayer. But it's him, all right. Beatrice's boyfriend. The one who laid him out in the garage. The one he sicked the two detectives on. Would he have recognized the man if he hadn't been thinking about Kayla and Beatrice?

These thoughts race through his mind in a split second. But they are powerful thoughts. Powerful enough to freeze his arm and hand, stop him from lifting the gun above the book and firing. Powerful enough to make his mouth blurt out, "You!"

*   *   *

Remi hates this man, hates what he did to Beatrice, hates what he'd surely do to Kayla if he had the chance. Still, he knows the man, and he hesitates.

The millisecond drags on with him staring at the mayor and the mayor staring back. Then, before there's time for a single heartbeat, he feels his hand being lifted, the trigger leading his finger.

The next thing he knows, there's a hole in the mayor's head, right between his eyes, and a fat spray of blood, bone, and gray matter evacuates the back of his head at high velocity. In Wallace Brown's eyes, he sees an instantaneous progression of surprise, confusion, rage, and terror. Then nothing.

He stands for a while, staring at the mayor, still sitting in his chair, head back, mouth agape, eyes open and flat. And that hole. Why did he shoot him in the face instead of the heart?

He takes a step closer to the desk, sees the big square lump under the man's shirt. A bulletproof vest. But he didn't know that, when he fired.

He looks down at the gun, still in his hand. The papers say the weapon has a name. Mr. Smith. He thinks about asking the gun if it knew about the vest, but that'd be crazy.

It's only then that he notices the gun in Wallace Brown's hand. The mayor was expecting him! It was a setup.

"Deke."

*   *   *

Rizzo parks his car on 15th Street, next to the bike lane. It's after midnight now, and quiet. Two kids race by on bikes and a thin fifty-ish white man walks across JFK Boulevard, away from City Hall, but there's no one else around.

He calls the mayor's office, the private line he's not supposed to have the number for. The mayor will pick up and Rizzo will identify himself, tell Wallace to come down and open the door for him. The mayor will hem and haw, but he'll do it. They'll walk together to his office and he'll get down to business. *What's this I hear about you and Nick Loughead and the Tick Tock killer?* The mayor will be evasive, tell him he doesn't know anything about the killer or this Nick. They'll dance for a while, until he puts the pressure on, reminds the mayor of the time he saved the man, then a DA, from assault charges at Delilah's, persuading the dancer to forget about what happened in return for the mayor giving her some cash, paying the hospital and dental bills. Remind him of the time Wallace sent him and Stanley Lipinski, another detective, to beat up on his ex's current boyfriend. "Let's have it," he'll say and the mayor will come clean, admit to what's going to go down with Tick Tock.

But the mayor doesn't answer. The cellphone rings and rings. Rizzo puts it into his pocket and looks around. He's close to the door to the northwest tower. It'll be locked, of course, but he tries it anyway.

It's not locked.

"Oh shit." His cop hackles up, he pulls out his gun and races inside and up the stairs. He reaches a security door, which is a dead end for him, since he doesn't have an access card. He calls dispatch, explains the situation, calls for backup. Dials again and, "Flynn, get your ass down to City Hall. I think something's happened between the killer and the mayor."

"The mayor? Oh. That would be bad."

"Ya think?"

He hangs up, waits at the door until backup—including someone with an access card—shows up. He opens the door, races with the others down the hall to the mayor's suite. They stop cold in the doorway to the mayor's office, stare at Wallace Brown's two dead eyes, and the bright red hole between them.

A patrolman, looking at Rizzo, asks, "Why the gun?"

"He was waiting for the killer."

The patrolman looks confused.

"He knew Tick Tock was coming. He was lying in wait. Hiding his gun behind that Bible propped up on the bookstand. The idea was that the killer would walk in, thinking he'd catch the mayor off guard, but Wallace would be ready for him, fire before the killer knew he'd been set up."

"So, what happened?"

"He wasn't as ready as he thought he was."

Rizzo sees that the scene is making the patrolman queasy.

"This your first dead guy?"

The patrolman nods. "Do they always have their mouth open like that?"

"Just the politicians."

* * *

Rizzo walks across Dilworth Plaza, toward his car. He hears police sirens screaming, sees the flashing red and white lights racing toward City Hall from every direction, neck and neck with a legion of white news vans. Brakes screech and cops, reporters, and cameramen leap from their vehicles, the cops running toward the building, the jackals positioning themselves on the plaza.

He glances toward JFK and stops in his tracks. The fifty-something! The one he saw walking just before he went into City Hall. It was the same guy outside the church that day he took his mother to see Father Kane, the priest looking at the guy with concern on his face. Something about the guy had looked familiar, made his cop hackles go up.

He closes his eyes, stands and thinks, the mayhem of the newsmen and cops fading into the background. And it hits him: *It was the same guy Wallace Brown sicked me and Lipinski on!*

What was his name? There was something odd about it. A weird nickname or something. Come on, what was his name? What was his name? What . . .

"Remi Bone."

He opens his eyes and dashes for his car. Pulling from the curb, he calls dispatch, yells into his microphone, "I need the address for a Remington Bohne."

* * *

Three blocks away, Nick Loughead paces his office above Kiddie Karate. Police cars speed past his building. The deed has been done, Tick Tock is dead, and the mayor's called the cops. But he was supposed to phone Nick first. Why hasn't he?

Nick figures the man must simply have forgotten in the heat of the moment. Fog of war, and all that. But he can't just stand there and wait.

Four minutes later, he crosses JFK to Dilworth Plaza. He's never seen so many cops and cop cars before, so many reporters and news vans. It doesn't surprise him, given the killer's notoriety, and all the problems he'd come to symbolize.

Nick makes his way toward a trio of cops standing guard in front of the West Gate. He walks closer, trying to act casual, just a regular citizen curious about what's going on.

"What's happening?" he asks.

The biggest of the cops looks at his colleagues, decides it's okay to tell him.

"The mayor's been shot. He's dead."

Nick Loughead balls his fists, closes his eyes, bends forward at the waist. And screams.

CHAPTER FIFTY-SIX

REMI SITTING IN his truck in the Rite Aid parking lot on Baltimore Avenue. He leans forward, his hands side-by-side around the top of the steering wheel, his forehead on his hands.

"No, no, no."

They'd set him up to die, Deke and the guy he was working with. They see him as a loose end, a dog needs putting down before he bites them in the ass.

And the mayor? Why'd he go along with it? But Remi knows the answer: To be a hero by killing the killer, saving the city from its boogeymen, old Tick Tock and his sidekick, Mr. Smith.

He feels the sledgehammer pounding in his chest, not feeling at all like something weak and dying. Maybe that shit Chuckie was wrong, after all. Maybe he just made it all up, told him his ticker was all ticked out to scare him, to get even for the beatings when they were kids. But he knows that's not the case, his always being tired and out of breath, the swelling in his feet and ankles, and that terrifying episode where he passed out, all telling him that Chuckie was telling the truth.

So, what is he going to do? That's the question. Should he shoot Deke? Or scare him into revealing who he's working with, find the guy, and shoot them both?

"No. No more."

He's done with it. And now that he's done with it, he's starting to feel sick about it.

"I mean, *what the hell?*" He lifts his head, pounds the steering wheel with both hands. *Killing people?*

He thinks some more, then decides to go to the garage, knowing, somehow, that Deke is still there. He'll confront the man, get him to admit he'd set him up, make him understand there was no cause for it. Everybody needed dying is dead; everybody still alive is going to stay that way.

*   *   *

Butch Kane still in his priest suit, watching TV, waiting for the news to hit the air. It happens about twelve thirty, the station cutting in right at the end of Jimmy Fallon. The newsman, some stand-in for anchorman Jim, now home in bed, tells the tale, the scene at City Hall playing out behind him.

He lowers his head, closes his eyes, heartsick at having failed the man, Remi Bone, a kid from school, grown up to become a husband and a father and now a cold-blooded killer. Failed to get through to him, steer him back onto the right path. Failed to save him and, in doing so, failed God, too.

The priest opens his eyes, decides what he has to do. Go to Remi's house, talk to the man one last time. Maybe get through to him, the man's sin so fresh it must be gnawing at him, at some level.

It takes him less than five minutes to reach the place. He climbs the steps, knocks on the door, even though he knows Remi's not home because his truck isn't in the driveway. He turns back to the street, just in time to see the sedan screech to a stop in front of the house.

He recognizes the driver as soon as he exits the vehicle, and he sees that the driver recognizes him, too.

"You knew it!" Rizzo shouts, advancing toward him. "He's the goddamned Tick Tock and you knew it all along!"

"I tried to save him."

"Yeah? What about all the people he shot? You try to save them? All it would'a taken was a phone call."

"I'm a priest. You know I can't divulge—"

"You still want to save him? Well now's your chance. If it's not too late."

He looks at the detective.

"He shot the mayor tonight, but it wasn't supposed to go down that way. It was a setup. The mayor was armed, and waiting for him."

"Oh, no."

"Tell me who was in it with him so I can find him before they do. Or maybe what I should ask is for you to help me find them before he does, since he surely knows he was set up, and he'll be gunning for them."

He thinks for a minute, then, "Come on," he says, brushing past the detective, running for the car.

CHAPTER FIFTY-SEVEN

DEKE BUFORD SEES the headlights in the compound, and his heart begins to race. He'd gotten off the phone with Nick only a few minutes earlier. Something had gone wrong with the mayor and now he was dead and Remi was out there, most likely knowing he'd been set up and looking for revenge. Apparently, the thing between Wallace Brown and Remi had happened some time ago, but Nick had waited to call, too upset to be thinking clearly. All of which left him with no time to flee.

He leans over, opens a drawer, and pulls out his Colt .380 Mustang. He releases the safety, points the gun through his open office door. He'll have a clean shot at Remi as soon as he opens the front door. The first shot may not put Bone down, but it'll hurt like hell and knock him off balance so that Deke will be able to advance and shoot him with little chance of accurate return fire.

He hears Remi's truck door close and starts taking quick, deep breaths.

* * *

Remi closes the driver's-side door and tucks the gun in the back of his pants. He feels more tired than he's ever felt before in his life.

But he's glad the killing is over, and that gives him the energy to move forward. He'll confront Deke, make the man confess to setting him up, then tell him the killing is done. Wanting no more to do with the gun, he'll give it to Deke and put the burden on him to get rid of it.

He opens the front door, takes a step inside, and hears the blast.

Straight ahead forty feet away, standing in the doorway to his office, is Deke, holding out a pistol.

Instinctively, he pulls Mr. Smith from behind him. But instead of raising the gun and firing, he closes his eyes and keeps moving forward. *No more killing. No more killing. I'm done.*

*   *   *

Deke fires again, his hand shaking even worse than the first time.

"Damn it."

Deke lifts his left hand, uses it to steady the right, and fires a third time. Still, Remi keeps moving forward, unscathed, his gun held down at his side, his eyes closed.

"Come on, come on," Deke orders himself, trying to steady his nerves.

He fires a fourth round, then a fifth, trying to concentrate on what he's doing, but his mind taking him back to that day on the track, when he was neck and neck with Richard Petty going into the last turn before the checkered flag, and his hands began to shake on the wheel because there was so much adrenaline flooding into his system and because Petty, that prick, was crowding him, and he crashed into the wall.

He fires again.

"Son-of-a-bitch!"

*   *   *

Remi's eyes are still closed, but he can hear Deke cursing, hear the panic rising in his voice. He keeps walking forward, knowing he'll soon be close enough that the man won't be able to miss despite himself, knowing he's a dead man. But not caring anymore, so tired of it all, so sick of it all.

He hears another shot and Deke stops cursing. He opens his eyes in time to see Deke fall to the floor, blood spurting from a hole in the center of his chest. He wonders what happened until he sees the gun, Mr. Smith, at the end of his raised arm.

The sight confuses him because he never made the decision to lift the gun, or to pull the trigger. The word *how?* forms in his mind, but before he has the time to figure out the answer, he hears the voice behind him.

*   *   *

"Put down the gun!"

Rizzo, his arms extended, service pistol in his right hand, left hand up to steady it, stands just inside the front door. Ahead of him, the Tick Tock killer, Remi Bone, facing toward the crumpled body of Deacon Buford. On the floor next to Buford, a pistol. Spurting from the hole in Buford's chest, blood.

"I said, put down the gun!"

The killer turns, lowers his right arm.

"Now, drop it."

But the killer doesn't move, just stands there, looking at him, then looking at the priest, now walking up behind Rizzo.

"I told the detective, Remi," Rizzo hears the priest say over his shoulder. "About your heart, about Kayla getting into Penn."

"Drop. The. Gun." Rizzo is starting to feel edgy, Mr. Smith still firmly in the grip of the killer, a murderer known to have the steely nerve and dead-eye accuracy to shoot his victims through the center of the heart. Or, right between the eyes when the vic wears a bulletproof vest, like the mayor.

"Remi, please," says Father Kane. "Do what he says. Let go of the gun."

The killer slowly shakes his head. "Can't let myself be arrested. Can't let Kayla find out about me."

"She's going to find out, whatever happens here." Rizzo inches his way toward the killer.

"You could let me go."

"You know I can't do that."

"I'm done killing. I won't hurt nobody else."

"Doesn't matter. You have to answer for what you've already done."

The killer smiles sadly. "That's going to happen soon enough, you take me in or not."

"Congestive heart failure," says the priest, now standing beside him. "Just like I told you."

"Chuckie Paxton says it could be any time now," the killer adds.

"Look, I don't know who Chuckie Paxton is—"

"He's the cardiologist," the priest says.

"I don't give a shit. Drop the gun!"

*   *   *

Butch Kane inches his way forward, so that he, Remi, and the detective form a triangle, with him off to the side, on Remi's right and the detective's left. He has a clear view now of both men's faces.

Remi's eyes are wells of despair.

In the detective's eyes, he sees growing impatience. And anger. Rizzo's face is wet with sweat, and he keeps glancing down at the gun in Remi's hand.

* * *

Remi looks first at the detective, then at Father Butch. "You were right," he tells the priest. "About remorse. I wish I could go back in time, change it all. Make so it never happened."

"Are you sorry because you're caught, Remi? Or is it something else?"

He looks at Butch Kane, the priest's face somehow soft and hard as iron at the same time. Remi looks within himself for the answer.

"The getting caught is there, but that's not all of it. Not even most of it." He takes a deep breath, feels his head sinking into his shoulders. "I can see the faces of all those men. I didn't feel nothing when I pulled the trigger. But I'm feeling it now."

"He'll know if you're bullshitting, Remi. Even if it's just you you're trying to fool, slapping a coat of remorse over your heart, so you can tell yourself you're a good guy after all."

"It's way too late for that, Butch. I got the violence in me, just like my daddy said. I'm bad to the core, and I know it."

"Enough!" It's the detective now. "You two can work this out in the confession booth."

Watching the man talk, Remi knows him now. "I remember you. You was one of them that Wallace Brown sicked on me after I laid him out for hitting Beatrice."

He sees the cop lick his lips, shift his glance between Remi's face and his gun, the famous Mr. Smith.

"Yes, that was me. And I'm sorry about that. I did some bad things, back when I was drinking. I owe a lot of apologies, and I'm giving one right now, to you. Now, please, put down the gun."

Remi glances at Butch Kane, who says, "Do it, Remi."

He turns back to the detective, who says, "I need to put you under arrest."

He nods. Then, rubbing Mr. Smith's grip, he shakes his head. "There's another way."

*   *   *

Kayla, in the back seat next to Charlene, both of them asleep, Charlene's mother at the wheel. Kayla had left her car at the high school, but by the time the bus pulled in, she was too tired to drive, tired from the basketball game and from the three-hour trip home. So she'd bummed a ride to her house from Charlene.

The car pulls up and she lifts her head, looks out the window, and is suddenly wide awake. It's after one a.m., and Remi's truck is nowhere to be seen.

She purses her lips, thanks Charlene and her mom, and stomps across the front yard, up the steps and into the house. The lights are out.

"This is bullshit," she says. Whatever he's been up to, he's at it again. She reaches into her jeans for her car keys, determined to go find him, then realizes her car is back at school.

Pulling her phone from her back pocket, she dials Virgil's personal cell number and waits for him to answer. She's met him twice for burgers and shakes, and they're developing a real friendship. At twenty-three, he's a little too old for her, and way too nerdy, but he's very smart and knows a lot and that makes him interesting to talk to.

Fifteen minutes later, she's seated beside him in his gleaming new Yukon, Virgil having moved up to Uber Black. "Let's start with the garage," she says. "He better be there."

Virgil gives her a look.

"What? What was that look?"

"I didn't know I gave you a look."

"Don't give me that line. You know what's going on all the time. I've watched you. There's little that other people do that gets past you, and nothing you do that you're not aware of."

He smiles. "You're very perceptive."

"Speed it up."

He presses down on the gas pedal, and she feels the SUV accelerate. They make a turn, drive a bit, then turn again onto the street the garage is on.

She leans forward to take in the scene. "What are all these police cars doing here?"

CHAPTER FIFTY-EIGHT

TEN DAYS AFTER Rizzo called in the double-murder at Buford's Garage, and Remi Bone is being laid to rest. Ballistics confirmed that Deacon Buford and his employee Remington Bohne had been killed by the gun known as Mr. Smith, both men having been shot through the heart. The news media had run with that report in declaring the Tick Tock killer still on the loose and decrying the police for failing to apprehend him.

Standing by Remi Bone's grave, Father Kane gives his spiel from the Gospel of John about believers not perishing but having everlasting life. Rizzo reaches out for Sharon's hand. She looks at him, lets him take it, their first physical contact since the morning after Buford's Garage. When he told Sharon what had really gone down the night before, she threw up her hands and walked away, then refused even to talk to him for two days, being so upset at his covering up the identity of the notorious killer and how the killer had really died.

He'd tried to make her understand he'd done the right thing, to save the killer's daughter from a lifetime of pain. He even tried to convince her that Bone wasn't such a bad guy, which he didn't really believe himself, but that only enraged her more.

Rizzo watches the priest finish up, sprinkle holy water on the coffin, invite the small crowd of mourners to place their roses on the coffin. Kayla, the daughter, is first, followed by her friend, the clean-cut blond kid who sat next to her, patting her hands throughout the graveside service. They are followed by a couple of men Rizzo figures to be Bone's coworkers from the garage, and a woman who'd introduced herself as the sister of Bone's deceased wife, the woman having flown in from Atlanta. The last to place their roses were a handful of men and women Rizzo figures for neighbors of Kayla and her father.

He watches the crowd disperse, asks Sharon, "Mind if I have a minute, to talk to the priest?"

"Go ahead. I'll give you my handcuffs. Hook yourself up to him; I can take you both in together."

*　*　*

Sharon watches Rizzo amble over to the big priest, shakes her head at what they'd done—two lunkheads got suckered into doing the bidding of a murderer. She turns to the supposed justification for their crimes, the girl, Kayla. Tall and pretty, she is, and smart enough to get accepted into an Ivy League college.

Sharon approaches the girl, notices her boyfriend fading into the background as she gets closer.

"My condolences," she says, taking Kayla's hands in hers.

"Thank you. And thank you for coming."

The girl's grip is firm, confident, her voice steady, her eyes dry. Sharon is impressed by her self-possession.

"I'm Sharon Walker, Detective Rizzo's captain. He told me what happened."

"I noticed the two of you, together," Kayla says, the look on her face telling Sharon the girl knows she's a lot more than Rizzo's boss.

Sharon smiles.

"Your Rizzo was very good to me, at the scene," Kayla says. "He tried to stop me from going into the garage. But I pushed past him. I saw Remi on the floor, and I guess I kind of lost it. I don't remember much of what happened after that, except that he got me into his car, called Father Kane to come to the scene and sit with me until he could drive me home."

"He can do the right thing, when he puts his mind to it."

"Same with all of them, I'm coming to learn. Men. Like it's against their nature, but if they try hard enough, they'll find a way to be good."

"You seem to know a lot for someone so young."

"My mom died when I was twelve. She left it to me to take care of Remi. I thought I was doing a good job, until the end."

Sharon stares, not sure what to say.

"He was getting home late, making up excuses for where he'd been. One time he came back with booze on his breath. I thought he was hitting the hard stuff, and I was rough on him. Turns out, he was helping Rizzo try to catch the killer. They were friends from the old days, them and the priest, and Rizzo had a lead old Tick Tock might've been someone else from the neighborhood."

"Rizzo told you that?"

"Yes."

"Jesus."

"Don't worry, I'm not going to tell anyone. Rizzo said it was a secret, and needed to be kept that way. I guess I'm not telling you anything you don't already know."

Sharon glances at Rizzo, thinking she's going to brain the idiot as soon as she gets him alone.

"Are you going to stick with him?" Kayla asks.

"I'm thinking about it."

"Worried you'll have your hands full?"

"Oh yeah."

"It's a lot of work, raising an old man."

"So I'm finding out."

"But it's worth it, if they turn out okay."

Sharon chuckles. She's liking this kid more and more.

Kayla excuses herself, and Sharon watches her walk over to her young man. She turns to see Rizzo and Father Kane approaching her.

"A remarkable young woman, don't you think?" the priest asks.

She waits a beat, then, "I'm still pissed at you. Both of you."

"How do you think she'd be doing right now if she'd learned her dad was a killer? That he'd shot those men to raise money to put her through school?"

She doesn't answer.

The priest says, "He works in mysterious ways."

"So it was God's doing?"

"If you'd been there, seen what I saw, you'd know He was there, too."

"You saw what you wanted to see, Father."

"That's a fact. Doesn't mean it wasn't real."

She turns to Rizzo. "Where do you come down on this?"

He shrugs. "The timing . . . I mean . . . maybe."

Before Sharon can come back at him, the priest looks past her, says, "How are you doing?"

Sharon turns to see Kayla and her friend almost up to them.

"I'm doing okay, Father," Kayla says. "All things considered. Thank you for conducting the service. I know you had to get special permission, seeing as my family is Baptist and all. But Remi never liked our pastor, and you two were friends."

"It was an honor, Kayla."

"I thought I'd let you know—let you all know—that I've made a decision, about college."

* * *

Father Kane holds his breath. "Don't tell us you're not going." *Not after the terrible price paid, by so many people, to get you there.*

"Of course, I'm still going to college. I've just changed my mind about what I'm going to study. I was planning to get a business degree. Then go for my MBA."

"And now?" Sharon asks.

"I'm going into law enforcement."

The priest sees Rizzo and his captain exchange uncomfortable glances.

"After all that happened with Remi," Kayla explains, "him working with the police to catch the killer, giving his life for the cause, I figure I owe it to him. Plus, I think I'll be really good at it. I'll have to go somewhere other than Penn, of course, given the cost. But I'm okay with that."

Butch Kane glances at Rizzo, then tells Kayla, "Actually, you may be able to go the Ivy League route, after all. The church has a surprisingly large educational endowment, left by a parishioner years ago. If you decide to join our congregation, I'd be happy to steer it your way."

"There's also a police scholarship," Rizzo pipes in, "for kids looking to join the force. It gives special consideration to students of parents killed in violent crimes."

Kayla hesitates. "I'm honored, but, well, I'm thinking more of going with the FBI than the local police."

Sharon holds her breath. *In for a penny.* "Not a problem. The scholarship is earmarked for those looking to join any agency of law enforcement."

"What is it they say?" asks Virgil, putting his arm around Kayla's shoulder. "When God closes a door, he opens a window."

*   *   *

Kayla glances from the big priest, to the fat detective, to the sexy police captain with the long red hair, people she never met or heard of just a few weeks ago, but now feeling to her like she's known them forever.

"*Casablanca*," she says.

They look at her, confused.

"I think this is the beginning of a beautiful friendship. A bunch of 'em."

CHAPTER FIFTY-NINE

"ANOTHER WAY?" Seeing the killer squeeze Mr. Smith, Rizzo tightens his grip on his Glock.

Remi nods down to the Smith & Wesson. "You take this gun. Use it on me. One shot, straight through the heart."

"I can't shoot you, unarmed. I'm a cop."

"You'd say you found me dead, with Deke here. Everyone will think old Tick Tock got us both."

"But you are the Tick Tock."

"But no one'll know it—Including my daughter."

The priest says, "Remi, you can't ask that of another man, not even for your daughter."

Rizzo listens as the killer ignores the priest, tells him, "Father, there's $95,000 in the toolbox on the back of my truck. You can use that to pay for Kayla's college. Just say it came from the church. Like a scholarship."

"It's not the right solution, Remi," says the priest.

"Why not? Everyone would get what they want. Tick Tock would be dead, so there'd be no more killing. You could take this Mr. Smith and throw it away. And Kayla would get to live her life as the daughter of a good man, not a murderer."

"But you are a murderer. And your plan would make *me* one, too," Rizzo says.

The killer falls silent, and the three of them stand for what seems to Rizzo like a month. Then, the killer's shoulders slump, his knees bend a little. The man is deflating.

Rizzo watches as the killer looks up at him, and drops the gun.

Rizzo lurches forward, retrieves the pistol from the floor, lays it on a toolbox beside him, and reaches for the killer. As he's about to lay hands on him, Bone's face becomes stricken with the most horrified look Rizzo's ever seen. The killer's eyes, focused not on Rizzo but something else, widen to the point of bulging. His mouth opens and turns down. A moan escapes from his throat.

And then, in an instant, the killer's face transforms again. The change is so dramatic Rizzo takes a step back.

His eyes glazed over, Remi Bone sits down on the floor, leans over, and dies.

Rizzo kneels, checks the man's pulse, looks up at the priest. "Did you see that awful look on his face?"

"Remorse," says Father Kane. "True remorse, if ever I saw it. What he was seeing was himself—the pitch-blackness of his own sins."

"And the second look?"

The priest smiles and tears form in the corners of his eyes. "A beatific smile. The rapture of forgiveness."

Rizzo studies the cleric, looking for signs of sarcasm. He finds none.

"Wait here," he says to the priest. "I have to go out to the car, call this in."

He's almost to the door when he hears the shot.

He spins around, sees the priest standing above the killer's corpse, holding the .38.

The priest looks back at him. "The Tick Tock killer strikes again."

"Jesus Christ."

"Not me, but in the building. Definitely in the building."

"The hell did you do?"

"Me? Nothing. Was the killer, got them both."

Rizzo stares at the priest for a full minute. Then he exhales. "You have to get out of here."

EPILOGUE

NICK LOUGHEAD CAN'T believe his luck. Everything is finally working out for him. He's never been so happy.

It hasn't come without a small price, of course. He's lost a little weight. Okay, more than a little. And his teeth keep falling out, not that he needs them since he doesn't really eat anymore. There are sores on his arms, but he enjoys picking at them, so that's not really a problem. There's a large abscess on his thigh, too, and he's fairly confident there's something alive inside his anus, but who cares, his life is pure bliss, and he's in love with the whole world.

It all started when that nice young man—the blond kid who always dresses like it's the 1950s—came to his office early in the morning, after the night when the city went insane with police sirens and lights. What was that all about? He can't remember. He does recall feeling afraid when the kid showed up, but he doesn't know why, the boy being so polite and concerned for his safety, and offering to hide him in his apartment—hide him from whom? He can't recall—which turned out not to be an apartment but a labyrinth of interconnected self-storage sheds in an abandoned facility near the airport. The kid kept him there for a day or two, or maybe it was a couple weeks, fed him, and gave him water that seemed to make him sleepy and then tied a rubber tube around his bicep and injected him with something that changed his life for-ever, something wonderful!

After a while, the boy said it was safe to leave and drove him to a place along the train tracks and helped him into the plywood and cardboard shack he lives in now. "I'll send someone to take care of you," the nice boy said, and he was true to his word because the very next day a guy showed up and injected him with the same stuff the kid had put into him, something that rushes up his arm in a series of tingles that explode into pure pleasure. The man, call-ing himself "the doctor," has been back every day since, always injecting him and bringing something for him to smoke in a glass tube that launches him like a rocket, something that makes him feel like a king. Like a *god*.

He doesn't know how long he'll be allowed to stay here, or what will happen once he's kicked out, but he doesn't care. He's so happy now, he doesn't think much about the future.

Through the darkness inside the cardboard shack, he senses movement. Sitting with his back against the plywood wall, he leans forward, sees the coal black eyes staring back at him.

"Hey, boy!" He smiles broadly at the black pit bull. His best friend going back as far as he can remember, which is about three weeks now. Or maybe three hours.

The dog glares at him, then lowers its head to smell his feet. It takes a lick, then a nibble, then Nick feels a pinching sensation and a yank, quite excruciating, actually, but who cares?

The dog starts to leave, then stops. It turns back to look at him, lifts his leg, sprays Nick's feet and ankles.

Nick smiles again and his eyes well up.

"I love you, boy. I love everybody."

* * *

Two hundred feet away, on the B Street Bridge between East Gurney Street and East Tusculum, stand four people, two women, two men. The younger woman is Lauren Devereux. The older woman is her new boss, Courtney Wilson, the former no-nonsense President of City Council, who had reluctantly assumed the mantle as the city's chief executive following Wallace Brown's assassination.

The two men are Conrail President Merle Hagee and Jefferson Cress, the railroad's chief legal officer. Both men are on the short side, with big bellies. Their suits are off the rack. Hagee has a crew cut. The thin strands of Cress's reddish hair are combed over the top of his head.

Mayor Wilson glances down at the deathscape of trash, broken furniture, needles, and barely moving bodies that is El Campamento, then turns to the two men. "I want that mess cleaned up as soon as possible."

"I don't think that's something we can do," Hagee says. "Right, Jeff?"

"It would be impossible to safely clean up the debris with all those people living along the tracks," the lawyer says. "Someone could get hurt. And we can't force them to move; that would be assault and battery. Only the police can legally assault people."

"I'm thinking three weeks should be enough time," Wilson says.

"Not to mention that our estimates show it would cost up to five million dollars to clear that area and fence it all off," Hagee says.

The mayor crosses her arms. "Make that two weeks."

"We're not making any headway here." Hagee shakes his head.

Mayor Wilson turns to Lauren. "Is the district attorney on his way?"

"He'll be here in about five minutes."

"District attorney?" Hagee pauses

"The way I see it," Wilson says, "with all the people dying up here, Conrail is guilty of homicide. Maybe not murder, but some level of homicide. I ran it by the DA and, I swear, he started salivating at the idea of prosecuting Conrail. You know he's planning to run for governor."

Hagee smiles. "You can't charge the railroad. We're a corporation. Corporations are never charged criminally. Everyone knows that."

"As chief counsel for the railroad," Jefferson Cress chimes in, "I should point out that Conrail doesn't actually exist. It's a legal fiction. Two other railroads own the rights to the *Conrail* name and they use it to run a little Ma and Pa operation here."

Courtney Wilson looks first to Cress then to Hagee. "You two seem real enough. And neither of you is a corporation. I'll tell the DA to charge you. Now which one of you is Ma and which is Pa?"

Lauren chuckles. Wallace Brown would never have had the smarts, or the balls, to play these two good old boys the way Mayor Wilson is doing now. Lauren is still smiling a moment later when she spots a black dog exit a cardboard shack next to the tracks below, climb the embankment to East Tusculum, and make its way toward them on the bridge. The men begin arguing with the mayor until they, too, notice the dog, and everyone stops.

"Is that a pit bull?" asks Jefferson Cress, who lives on the ritzy Main Line, where there are no such dogs.

"What's it have in its mouth?" asks Merle Hagee.

The dog advances toward them and Lauren answers. "If I'm not mistaken, it's a toe. A big toe. And it looks crooked." Prudently, she chooses not to tell them she's seen it before.

Merle Hagee's hand is to his chest in a heartbeat. "Jesus!"

The dog growls as it marches past them, and Mayor Wilson turns to the railroad men. "Where were we? Oh yes. Two weeks."

"I'll have the crews here first thing Monday," Hagee says.

"Start with that shack," Lauren says. "The one the dog came out of. Bulldoze it. Bulldoze it flat."

They talk some more, then the men walk away.

Lauren and the mayor watch them go and then turn and look down toward the railroad tracks.

"We have to end this," Wilson says. "And not just El Campamento, but all of it. The drugs are killing us."

They stand quietly for a few moments, until Lauren starts the couplet.

"Tick tock says the clock."

"Time's up, motherfuck."

ACKNOWLEDGMENTS

My appreciation begins with my wife, Lisa, for her support, encouragement, and, above all, her honesty—"Let's put this one in the drawer until you're famous." Without you, I never would have begun this journey.

Many thanks to my indulgent early readers and friends Jill SHS Reiff, Neil Reiff, Alan Sandman, Rob Sinnamon, Andrea Sinnamon, Naumon Amjed, Lauren Amjed (the only one who got that the gun pointed itself), Greg Cunningham, and Jill Cunningham. Thanks also to my law school classmate and friend Paul Shapiro for sharing George V. Higgins' seminal crime novel *The Friends of Eddie Coyle*, which, along with Elmore Leonard's books, was an inspiration for *Remi Bone*.

To my agent, Cynthia Manson, who never quits, and who helped me bring this quirky book to life.

Thank you to Bob and Pat Gussin, Faith Matson, Lee Randall, and the whole team at Oceanview. You've built a great publishing house and are truly fun to work with!

My special thanks to Oceanview for designing a cover that perfectly captures the mood and essence of this quirky tale, proving that sometimes you really can judge a book by its cover.

Finally, to all of the readers who will choose *Remi Bone*. I had a blast penning this tale and I hope you enjoy it. Whatever you think, please let me know.

www.williamlmyersjr.com

 @WilliamMyersJr

 WilliamLMyersJr

 @Jr.WilliamMyers

PUBLISHER'S NOTE

We hope that you enjoyed *REMI BONE* and suggest that you read William L. Myers, Jr.'s previous novel, *BACKSTORY,* a psychological thriller.

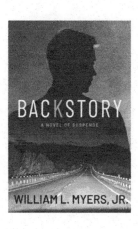

Jackson Robert Hunter, known to his local friends as "Bob," has been hit on the head and has lost his memory—his backstory. He knows his wife is dead, apparently by suicide; he cannot recall the surrounding circumstances but is convinced that she has been murdered—in retaliation for his own dark past, the past he had tried to escape living an "ordinary life" in the heartland.

"Taut, tense, and thrilling, *Backstory* traces the fault line between an amnesiac's violent past and his dangerous present. When the two collide, it's with the force of an earthquake."
—Hilary Davidson, best-selling author

We hope that you will enjoy reading *BACKSTORY* and that you will look forward to more to come.

For more information, please visit the author's website:
www.williamlmyersjr.com

If you liked *REMI BONE,* we would be very appreciative if you would consider leaving a review. As you probably already know, book reviews are important to authors and they are very grateful when a reader makes the special effort to write a review, however brief.

Happy Reading,
Oceanview Publishing
Your Home for Mystery, Thriller, and Suspense